A True Hero

W. H. G. Kingston

"A True Hero"

By

WHG Kingston

1872

Chapter One.

The Protectorate had come to an end ten years before the period when our story commences; and Charles the Second, restored to the throne of England, had since been employed in outraging all the right feelings of the people over whom he was called to reign, and in lowering the English name, which had been so gloriously raised by the wisdom of Cromwell. The body of that sagacious ruler of a mighty nation had been dragged out of its tomb among the kings in Westminster, and hanged on the gallows-tree at Tyburn; the senseless deed instigated by the petty revenge of his contemptible successor. The mouldering remains of Blake, also, one of the noblest among England's naval heroes, had been taken from its honoured resting-place, and cast into an unknown grave in Saint Margaret's churchyard. Episcopacy had been restored by those who hoped thus to pave the way for the re-introduction of Romanism, with its grinding tyranny and abject superstitions. The "Conventicle Act," prohibiting more than five persons, exclusive of the family, to meet together for religious worship according to any other than the national ritual, had been passed, and was rigidly enforced; the dominant party thus endeavouring to deprive the people of one of the most sacred rights of man, — that of worshipping God according to the dictates of conscience. England's debauched king, secretly a Papist, had sold his country for gold to England's hereditary foe, whose army he had engaged to come and crush the last remnants of national freedom, should his Protestant people dare to resist the monarch's traitorous proceedings. The profligacy and irreligion of the court was widely imitated by all classes, till patriots, watching with gloomy forebodings the downward progress of their country, began to despair of her future fate. Such was the state of things when, on the morning of the 14th of August, 1670, several sedate, grave-looking persons were collected at the north end of Gracechurch Street, in the City of London. Others were coming up from all quarters towards the spot. As the first arrived, they stood gazing towards the door of a building, before which were drawn up a body of bearded, rough soldiers, with buff coats, halberds in hand, and iron caps on their heads. Several of the persons collected, in spite of the armed men at the door, advanced as if about to enter the building.

"You cannot go in there," said the sergeant of the party; "we hold it in the name of the king. Begone about your business, or beware of the consequences!" In vain the grave citizens mildly expostulated. They received similar rough answers. By this time other persons had arrived, while many passers-by stopped to see what was going forward. Among those who came up was a tall young man, whose flowing locks and feathered cap, with richly-laced coat, and silk sash over his shoulder, to which, however, the usual appendage, a sword, was wanting, showed that he was a person of quality and fashion. Yet his countenance wore a grave aspect, which assumed a stern expression as he gazed at the soldiers. He stopped, and spoke to several of those standing round, inquiring apparently what had occurred. About the same time, another man, who seemed to be acquainted with many of the persons in the crowd, was making his way among them. He was considerably more advanced in life than the first-mentioned person, and in figure somewhat shorter and more strongly built. Though dressed as a civilian, he had a military look and air. From an opposite direction two other persons approached the spot, intending, it seemed, to pass by. The one was a man whose grizzly beard and furrowed features showed that he had seen rough service in his time, his dress and general appearance bespeaking the soldier. His companion was a youth of sixteen or seventeen years of age, so like him in countenance that their relationship was evident. From the inquiries they made, they were apparently strangers.

"Canst tell me, friend, what has brought all these people together?" said the elder man to a by-stander.

"Most of these people are 'Friends,' as they call themselves," answered the man addressed, a well-to-do artisan, "or 'Quakers,' as the world calls them, because they bid sinners exceedingly to quake and tremble at the word of the Lord. To my mind they are harmless as to their deeds, though in word they are truly powerful at times. The bishops and church people do not like them because they declare that God can be worshipped in the open air, or in a man's own home, as well as in the grandest cathedral, or 'steeple house,' as they call the church. The Independents are opposed to them, because they deem ministers unnecessary, and trust to the sword of the Spirit rather than to carnal weapons; while the wealthy and noble disdain them, because they refuse to uncover their heads, or to pay undue respect to their fellow-men, however rich or exalted in rank they may be. They have come to hold a meeting in yonder house, where the soldiers are stationed; but as speaking will not open the doors, they will have to go away again disappointed."

"If they are the harmless people you describe, that seems a hard case," observed the stranger. "By what right are they prohibited from thus meeting?"

"I know not if it is by right, but it is by law," answered the artisan. "You have doubtless heard of the 'Conventicle Act,' prohibiting all religious worship, except according to the established ritual. The 'Friends' alone hold it in no respect, and persist in meeting where they have the mind!"

"What! do all the other dissenters of England submit to such a law?" exclaimed the stranger.

"Marry do they," answered the artisan. "They pocket the affront, and conform in public to what is demanded, satisfying their consciences by worshipping together in private. Do you not know that every head of a family is fined a shilling on every Sunday that he neglects to attend the parish church? You can have been but a short time in England not to have heard of this."

"Yes, indeed, my friend. My son and I landed but yesterday from a voyage across the Atlantic; and, except from the master and shipmen on board, we have heard but little of what has taken place in England for some years past."

"Canst tell me, friend, what has brought all these people together!"

"Then take my advice, friend," said the artisan. "Make all the inquiries you please, but utter not your opinions, as you were just now doing to me, or you may find yourself accused of I know not what, and clapped into jail, with slight chance of being set free again."

"Thank you, friend," said the stranger; "but will all these people submit to be treated thus by those few soldiers? By my faith, it's more than I would, if I desired to enter yonder house of prayer."

While this conversation was going on, the number of people in front of the Quaker's meeting-house had greatly increased; and though the greater number appeared quietly disposed, there were evidently some hovering about, and others now elbowing their way through the crowd, who were inclined to create an uproar. At this juncture, the young gentleman who has already been described, stepping on one side of the street where the pavement was highest, took off his hat. "Silence, I pray you, dear friends; I would speak a few words," he said, in a rich musical voice. "We came here purposing to enter yonder house, where we might worship God according to the dictates of our consciences, and exhort and strengthen one another; but it seemeth to me that those in authority have resolved to prevent our thus assembling. We are men of peace, and therefore must submit rather than use carnal weapons; and yet, friends, having the gift of speech, and the power of the pen, we must not cease to protest against being thus deprived of the liberty which Englishmen hold so dear."

Chapter Two.

While the young man was speaking, the stranger and his son had worked their way close to the stout soldier-like man who has been described. The stranger's eye fell on his countenance. He touched his son's shoulder. "An old comrade in arms!" he whispered. "A truer man than Captain William Mead,—trusty Bill Mead, we used to call him,—never drew sword in the cause of liberty. If I can but catch his eye and get a grip of his honest hand, I will ask him who that young man can be,—a brave fellow, whoever he is." In another instant the two old comrades had recognised each other.

"What, Christison! Nicholas Christison! is it thou?" exclaimed Captain Mead, examining the stranger's countenance. "Verily, I thought thou wast no longer in the land of the living; but thou art welcome, heartily welcome. Come with me to my house in Cornhill, at the sign of the 'Spinning Wheel,' and thou shalt tell me where thou hast been wandering all this time; while, may be, we will have a talk of bygone days."

"With all my heart," answered Christison; "but tell me who is that noble youth addressing the people? He seems by his dress and bearing not one likely to utter such sentiments as are now dropping from his mouth!"

"Verily, he is not less noble in deed and word than in look," answered Mead. "He is William Penn, the son of the admiral who fought so well for the Commonwealth, and now serves a master about whom the less we say the better."

"I remember him well; a brave, sagacious man, but one who was ever ready to serve his own interest first, and those of his country afterwards. I should not have expected to find a son of his consorting with Quakers."

"No, verily; as light from darkness, so does the son differ from the father in spiritual matters," answered Mead. "The son has sacrificed all his worldly prospects for the sake of his own soul and for those of his fellow-creatures. In a righteous cause he fears no foes, temporal or spiritual; and is ready to lay down his life, if needs be, for the truth."

"A brave youth he must be, by my troth," observed Christison. "Wenlock, my boy, I pray Heaven you may be like him. I would rather have thee a thorough true-hearted man, than the first noble in the land."

At this moment, Mead, who had been stopped by the crowd from making his way towards the place where William Penn was speaking, saw an opportunity of advancing, and again moved forward, accompanied by his old friend and his son. There was, indeed, a general movement in the crowd, and voices in tones of authority were heard shouting, "Make way there; make way!" The people who uttered these cries were soon recognised as sheriffs' officers. They were advancing towards Penn. Their intention was evident.

"They are about to arrest him," said Mead; "but he has done nothing worthy of bonds."

"No, by my troth he has not," exclaimed Christison; "and I would gladly, even now, strike a blow for the cause of liberty, and rescue him from their power, if they attempt to lay hands on him."

"No, no, friend, put up thy sword," said Mead; "we fight not with carnal weapons. He would not thank you for any such attempt on your part."

By this time the constables had reached Penn, and informed him that he was their prisoner. Two others at the same time came up to where Mead was standing, and arrested him also. It was a sore trial to the old Republican officer to stand by and see his friend carried off to prison.

"By whose authority am I arrested?" asked Penn, turning with an air of dignity to the officers.

One of them immediately produced a document. "See here, young sir," he said in an insulting tone, "This is our warrant! It is signed by the worshipful Lord Mayor, Sir Samuel Starling. I have a notion that neither you nor any of your friends would wish to resist it."

"We resist no lawful authority; but I question how far this warrant is lawful," answered the young Quaker. "Howbeit, if thou and thy companions use force, to force we yield, and must needs accompany thee whithersoever thou conductest us."

"Farewell, old friend," said Mead, shaking Christison by the hand, as the constables were about to lead him off. "I would rather have spent a pleasant evening with thee in my house than have had to pass it in a jail: but yet in a righteous cause all true men should be ready to suffer."

"Indeed so, old comrade; and you know that I am not the man to desert you at a pinch. As we are not to pass the evening together at your house, I will spend it with you in jail. I suppose they will not exclude you from the society of your friends?"

Mead shrugged his shoulders. "It is hard to say how we may be treated, for we Quakers gain but scant courtesy or justice."

These last remarks were made as Mead, with a constable on either side of him, was being led off with William Penn to the Guildhall.

The old Commonwealth officer and his son followed as close behind them as the shouting, jeering mob would allow them; Christison revolving in his mind how he should act best to render assistance to his old friend. At length they arrived at the hall where the Lord Mayor was sitting for the administration of justice.

Captain Christison and his son entered with others who found their way into the court. A short, though somewhat corpulent-looking gentleman, with ferrety eyes and rubicund nose, telling of numerous cups of sack which had gone down between the thick lips below it, occupied the magisterial chair.

"Who are these knaves?" he exclaimed, in a gruff voice, casting a fierce glance at the young William Penn and his companion, Captain Mead. "What! ye varlets, do you come into the presence of the Lord Mayor of London with your hats on? Ho! ho! I know you now," he exclaimed, as an officer handed him a paper, while he turned his eyes especially on Penn. "Let me tell you, if you pay not proper respect to the court, I will have you carried to Bridewell and well whipped, you varlet, though you are the son of a Commonwealth admiral! Do you hear me, sirrah?"

"By my troth," whispered Christison to his son. "I should like to rush in with my sword and stop that foul-speaking varlet's mouth, Lord Mayor of London though he be. And now I look at him, I remember him well, Master Starling, a brawling supporter of the Protector when he was seated firmly at the head of Government. And now see, he is louder still in carrying out the evil designs of this Charles Stuart and his myrmidons." These words, though said in a low voice, were not altogether inaudible to some of the by-standers.

"Beware!" said some one at his elbow.

To this tirade of the Lord Mayor, the young gentleman made no answer. "Do you hear me, sirrah?" he exclaimed again; "I speak to you, William Penn. You and others have unlawfully and tumultuously been assembling and congregating yourselves together for the purpose of creating a disturbance of the peace, to the great terror and annoyance of His Majesty's liege people and subjects, and to the ill example of all others; and you have, in contempt of the law of the land, been preaching to a concourse of people whom you tumultuously assembled for the purpose of instigating them to rebel against His Majesty the king and the authorities of this city of London."

"Verily, thou art misinformed and mistaken, sir," answered the young man, in a calm voice. "I neither created a disturbance, nor did I utter words whereby any disturbance could have been created, while I have ever been a loyal and dutiful subject of King Charles as His Majesty."

"Ho! ho! ho! you have come here to crow high, I warrant you," exclaimed Sir Samuel Starling; "and your companion, Master Mead, will, I warrant, declare himself equally innocent of offence!"

"Thou speakest truly, friend," answered Captain Mead; "I was the cause of no disturbance, as all those present very well know; for no disturbance indeed took place, while my principles forbid me to oppose the authorities that be."

These calm answers only seemed to enrage Sir Samuel Starling, who, heaping further abuse on the prisoners, exclaimed, "Take the varlets off to the 'Black Dog' in Newgate Market; there they shall remain in durance till they are tried for their crimes at the Old Bailey, and we shall then see whether this young cock-of-the-woods will crow as loudly as he now does."

Young Wenlock could with difficulty restrain his father's indignation when he heard this order pronounced by the city magistrate. He however, managed to get him out of the court.

"We will go and see where they are lodged, at all events," said the captain, who at length yielded to his son's expostulation. "Perchance I may render my old friend Mead, and that noble young fellow Penn, some assistance."

Chapter Three.

In a dirty, ill-ventilated room in a low sponging-house in Newgate Market, known as the "Black Dog," two persons were seated. Cobwebs hung from the windows and the corners of the ceiling, occupied by huge, active spiders, lying in wait for some of the numerous flies which swarmed on the dust-covered panes. On the walls were scrawled numerous designs, executed by the prisoners who had from time to time occupied the room, to while away their hours of durance. The air felt close and sultry, the heat increased by the rays of the sinking sun, which found their way in by the window, through which also entered unpleasant odours ascending from the court-yard below. One of the persons, whose handsome dress contrasted strangely with the appearance of the room, was busy writing at a rickety table. With youth, wealth, talents, a fair fame, the godson of the future monarch of England, he might, had he so willed, have been a peer of he realm, the founder of a noble family. The other, who has been described as Captain Mead, rose from his seat, and walked up and down with somewhat impatient steps. "I am writing to my dear father to tell him the cause of my absence," said young Penn, stopping for a moment. "I fear that his sickness is very serious, and deep is my regret to be kept away from him; yet do I glory in thus suffering for the great and noble principles for which we are striving,—liberty of conscience, liberty of action. What is life worth to man without these? And yet our infatuated countrymen run a great risk of losing both, if they refuse to listen to the voice of warning, and to prepare in time for the threatened danger." Just then a turnkey opened the door, and in an impudent tone of voice said, "Here's a man and a lad come to see Master Mead. There, go in and sit as long as you please, till the hour arrives when all visitors must be turned out."

"Ah! friend Christison and thy fine boy, thou art welcome to this our somewhat sorry abode," said Mead. "I would rather have seen thee at my family board this evening, as I had proposed; but we must submit to the powers that be. I will now make thee known to our friend Master William Penn, whose father thou and I served under in days gone by."

"Ay, marry, I remember him well!" exclaimed Christison. "We were with him when he chased that piratical, malignant Rupert, and well-nigh caught him. Many a rich argosy would have been preserved to the Commonwealth had we succeeded; but the devil favours his children, and the rover got off."

"We will not now speak of those times," said Mead. "I am not surprised to hear thee, old comrade, allude to them thus; but I, now taught better, have laid aside the use of carnal weapons."

"Well, well, I know you will always do as your conscience dictates," said Christison; "and gladly do I shake hands with the son of my old commander."

William Penn rose, and courteously welcomed the visitor, giving a kind smile and a touch on the shoulder to young Wenlock. "Let my presence not interfere with you, friend," he said; "but as thou seest I am busily engaged in writing on matters of importance; thou mayst talk state secrets to each other, and I shall not hear them; so, pray thee, Master Christison, make thyself at home with thy old friend." Saying this, he resumed his seat and continued writing, completely absorbed in his work. Captain Mead warmly thanked his old friend for coming to see him.

"And what is it I hear of you," asked Christison; "that you have joined the followers of George Fox?"

"Verily, I have deserted all worldly systems, and have united with those who believe that the guidance of the Spirit is sufficient to lead us into all truth: the Holy Scriptures being the only fit and outward rule whereby to judge of the truth. I pray thee, old friend, do not strive against that Holy Spirit, a measure of which has surely been given to thee. That is the light and life of the Holy Word which 'in the beginning was with God, and was God.' That it is which will enlighten thy mind, if thou strivest not to quench it."

In a similar strain Mead continued putting forth and explaining to his old friend the doctrine held by the Quakers. He spoke to him of the unity of the Godhead. "We believe," he added, "that their light is one, their life one, their wisdom one, their power one; and that he that knoweth and seeth any one of them knoweth and seeth them all, as our blessed Lord says, 'He that hath seen me hath seen the Father.' We believe, too, though most wrongfully accused of the contrary, that God the Son is both God and man in wonderful union; that He suffered for our salvation, was raised again for our justification, and ever liveth to make intercession for us. He is that Divine Word that lighteth the souls of all men that come into the world with a spiritual and saving light, as none but the Creator of souls can do. With regard to our worship, we hold that 'God is a Spirit, and desires to be worshipped in spirit and in truth,' not only on one day, but on all days of the week; not only when meeting together, but in the daily concerns of life; and the man who worships not then, will render poor worship when he assembles with his fellow-men at the time he may think fit to set apart for that purpose. As we acknowledge no other Mediator than the Son of God, who came on earth and died for our sins, and, having risen from the grave and ascended into heaven, is now seated at the right hand of God; so we require no person to pray for us, or allow that it is according to God's will that persons should receive payment for praying, exhorting, or preaching, or in any other way spreading God's truth. We believe, too, that the water-baptism, so generally administered, is not according to God's mind; that the baptism spoken of in the Scriptures is that of the Spirit, — the answer of a good conscience towards God by the resurrection of Jesus Christ; that by one Spirit we are all baptised into one body; while, with regard to the Lord's Supper as it is spoken of, we do indeed deem that the supper of the Lord is needful, but that it is altogether of a spiritual nature. We object altogether to oaths, because our Lord says, 'Swear not at all.' We hold war to be an abomination to God, and contrary to that new commandment given us by Christ, 'That ye love one another, even as I have loved you.' We hold, too, that a civil magistrate has no right to interfere in religious matters, and that though 'Friends' may admonish such members as fall into error, it must be done by the spiritual sword; and as religion is a matter solely between God and man, so no government consisting of fallible men ought to fetter the consciences of those over whom they are placed."

"No, indeed," exclaimed Christison. "To the latter principle I have long held; and it seems to me that there is much sense and truth in the other tenets which you have explained. I, as you know, am a blunt man, not given to book learning; but, in truth, old friend, I should like to hear from you again more at large of these matters."

"There seems every probability that thou wilt know where to find me for some time to come," answered Mead; "and I shall be heartily well-pleased further to explain to you the principles we hold to be the true ones for the guidance of men in this mortal life."

"Father," said young Wenlock, as he and the elder Christison were returning to their lodgings; "I should like to take service with young Master Penn, should he require a secretary. Your old friend, Captain Mead, has also taken my fancy; but yet I feel I would go anywhere with so true-hearted and noble a man as the other."

"You have formed a somewhat hasty judgment, Wenlock," said his father. "We have been but a couple of hours in his society, during which time he spoke but little; and though, I grant you, he is a true gentleman, and would have made a fine soldier, yet his temper and habits may be very different to what you suppose."

"Oh! no, no, father. I know I could trust him; I watched him all the time he was writing. He said he was addressing his father, and I saw his change of countenance; sometimes he was lost in thought, sometimes he seemed to look up to heaven in prayer; and more than once I saw his eyes filled with tears, and a firm, determined look came over his countenance; yet all the time there was nothing stern or forbidding,—all was mild, loving, and kind. I have never seen one I would more willingly serve."

"I hope that you may see him frequently, Wenlock," said his father, "and you may thus have an opportunity of correcting or confirming your judgment. I purpose visiting my old friend Mead whenever I can."

Captain Christison kept to his word. The result of those frequent interviews with the worthy Quaker, as far as Wenlock was concerned, will be shown by-and-by.

The first of September, 1670, the day fixed for the trial of William Penn and Captain Mead, arrived, and the prisoners were placed in the dock to answer the charge brought against them. Christison and his son were at the doors some time before they opened, that they might, without fail, secure a place. "Now most of these people, I warrant, fancy that they have come simply to witness the trial of the son of one of England's brave admirals for misdemeanour. The matter is of far more importance, Wenlock. Master Penn disputes, and so do I, that this 'Conventicle Act' is legal in any way. We hold it to be equally hostile to the people and our Great Charter. Is an edict which abolishes one of the fundamental rights secured to the nation by our ancient Constitution, though passed by Crown and Parliament, to be held as possessing the force of law? If this court cannot show that it is, the question is, will a jury of Englishmen, when the case is made clear to them, venture to convict?"

On entering the hall they found ten justices occupying the bench, Sir Samuel Starling, the Lord Mayor, at their head. As soon as the court opened, the clerk ordered the crier to call over the jury. Having answered to their names, of which the result showed that they had every reason to be proud, they were sworn to try the prisoners at the bar, and find according to the evidence adduced. If Wenlock had been inclined to admire William Penn before, much more so was he now, when, standing up, he replied to the question whether he was guilty or not guilty. Of course he and Mead pleaded not guilty. The court then adjourned. After it had resumed its functions the prisoners were brought up, but were set aside in order that several cases of common felony might be disposed of; this being done for the purpose of insulting Penn and his friend. Little progress having been made in their case, they were remanded to their abominable dungeons in Newgate, and the court adjourned for two days.

Chapter Four.

Christison and his son arrived in good time when the court again sat, on the 3rd of September. The officers having taken off the hats of the prisoners as they entered, the Lord Mayor abused them for so doing, and bade them put them on again. He then abused the prisoners for wearing their hats, fining them forty marks each for contempt of court. The indictment was again read. It was to the effect that William Penn and William Mead, with other persons, had assembled on the 15th day of August for the purpose of creating a disturbance, according to an agreement between the two; and that William Penn, supported by William Mead, had preached to the people assembled, whereby a great concourse of people remained, in contempt of the king and his law, creating a disturbance of his peace, to the great terror of many of his liege people and subjects.

William Penn, who ably defended himself, proved that the day when he had gone to Gracechurch Street was the fourteenth, and not the fifteenth; that he did not preach to the people; that he had not agreed to meet William Mead there; that William Mead had not spoken to him. Mead also proved that he had not preached; that he had not abetted Penn, and that no riot had taken place.

Contrary to the evidence, the Recorder Jefferies insisted that the prisoners should be brought in "guilty." The jury, however, in spite of the threats held out to them by the Lord Mayor and the Recorder and others, would not agree upon a verdict. The most determined to give an honest one was Master Edward Bushel, whose name deserves to be recorded. On again being compelled to retire, they were absent for some time. When they once more returned, the foreman announced that their verdict was "Guilty of speaking in Gracechurch Street." Again every effort was made to induce them to pronounce a different verdict. A third time they were ordered to retire. Again, in writing, they handed in their verdict, finding William Penn "Guilty of speaking to an assembly in Gracechurch Street," and acquitting William Mead.

The baffled and beaten bench, now losing temper, ordered the jury to be locked up, and the prisoners to be taken back to Newgate. Penn, now addressing them, required the clerk of the peace to record their verdict. "If, after this," he exclaimed, "the jury bring in a different verdict to this, I affirm that they are perjured men. You are Englishmen," he said, turning to the jurors. "Remember your privileges. Give not away your rights!"

The following day was Sunday. They were called up, however, and the clerk again inquired if they were agreed. The foreman replied as before, "Guilty of speaking to an assembly in Gracechurch Street."

"To an unlawful assembly?" exclaimed the Lord Mayor.

"No, my lord," answered the noble Master Bushel. "We give no other verdict than we gave last night."

In vain the Lord Mayor and the Recorder Jefferies threatened as before; the Lord Mayor shouting out, "Gaoler, bring fetters, and shake this pestilent fellow to the ground!"

"Do your will," answered Penn; "I care not for your fetters!"

The Recorder Jefferies now cried out, "By my troth, I could never before understand why the Spaniards suffered the Inquisition among them; and, to my mind, it will never be well with us in England till we have among us something like the Inquisition."

"Boy," whispered Christison to his son, "you heard those words. The knave has a good idea of his master's notions and designs. If the Inquisition,—and I know something of it,—is ever established in this fair England of ours, it must either be quickly driven out again, or our country will be no fit place for honest men."

Once more the jury were locked up, without food, fire, or water; but they were Englishmen to the backbone, and were ready to die in the cause of civil freedom, rather than play traitors to their own convictions.

On Monday the court again sat. Each juror was separately questioned, and one and all pronounced "Not guilty." The Recorder on this fined them forty marks a man, and imprisonment in Newgate till the fines were paid. Penn and Mead were fined in the same way, the Recorder crying out, "Put him out of court! Take him away!"

"'Take him away!'" exclaimed Penn. "Whenever I urge the fundamental laws of England, 'Take him away!' is their answer; but no wonder, since the Spanish Inquisition sits so near the Recorder's heart."

Both prisoners and jurors were carried off to Newgate, refusing to pay the fines: Penn and Mead as a case of conscience; while Bushel advised his fellow-jurors to dispute the matter. The jurors were committed to prison on the 5th of September, and it was not till the 9th of November that the trial came on. Learned counsel were engaged for their defence; Newdegate, one of them, arguing that the judges may try to open the eyes of the jurors, but not to "lead them by the nose." Christison and his son were present. "I had hoped to spend some years in my native land, and renew the friendship I formed in my youth," observed the former; "but I tell thee, Wenlock, if this trial goes against those twelve honest men, I will forswear my country, and go and seek thy fortune and mine in some other land, where knaves do not, as here, 'rule the roost.'" When, however, the twelve judges gave an almost unanimous verdict in favour of the jurymen, Christison agreed that, after all, there were more honest men in the country than he had feared was the case.

To return, however, to William Penn and Mead. They were remanded to Newgate, refusing to pay the fines imposed on them, as a matter of conscience. Without difficulty, Christison and Wenlock obtained admittance to them. "Truly, friends, you are hardly dealt with," said the former, as he shook hands. "We had tyrannical proceedings enough in the time of the first Charles, but it seems to me that we are even worse off now. I would that I could collect a band of honest fellows and rescue you out of this vile den."

"I pray thee, be silent, dear friend," said Mead. "We are here for conscience sake; and our consciences being right towards God, would support us under far greater trial."

"Well, well, I suppose you are right," answered Christison; "but it sorely troubles me to see you here. I came back to England, understanding that the country was enjoying rest, and prospering under the new reign; but it seems to me that the rest is more that of wearied sleep than prosperous tranquillity, and that ere long the people will revive, and will once more draw the sword to reassert their rights."

"I pray not," said Mead; "but I do pray that those principles which I have unfolded to thee, old friend, may be promulgated throughout the length and breadth of England; as it is through them, and them only, that the country can obtain true rest, and prosper as a Christian people would desire."

Two days after this, the prisoners were pacing their cell, talking earnestly on matters seldom discussed within prison walls, when the turnkey entered.

"Gentlemen," he said, "I bring you news such as may perhaps be satisfactory. Your fines have been paid, and you are at liberty to depart from hence. I trust you will not forget the attention and courtesy with which I have treated you!"

"Verily, knave!" exclaimed Mead, laughing as Quakers were not wont to laugh, "thou ought to go to Court and push thy fortune there. I would willingly pay thee for all the attention thou hast shown us, but I fear thou wouldst not be satisfied with the payment. If I give thee more than thy deserts, thou wilt be better pleased. Here, take this groat. Art thou satisfied?"

The turnkey made a wry face, and Mead followed Penn, who had hurried out, anxious to be free from the prison. On the outside they met Christison and Wenlock, with several other friends, waiting for them. Penn hastened to his lodgings to change his dress, requesting

Mead to order horses directly, that he might proceed down to his father.

"Come," said Mead to his old comrade; "many days have passed since I gave thee an invitation to my abode; but as I have not since then been a free agent, I could not have received thee as I desired."

Chapter Five.

Wenlock Christison and his son proceeded up Cornhill a short time after the events which have been described. They were examining the various signs over the shop doors, in search of that which distinguished Master Mead's abode.

"Ah! there it is," said Wenlock; "that must be the 'Spinning Wheel' he told us of."

A demure youth with well-brushed hair was standing at the door, in courteous language inviting passers-by to enter and inspect his master's goods.

"Is this Master Mead's abode, young man?" inquired Captain Christison.

"Verily, friend, it is," answered the shopman. "If thou wilt enter, thou wilt find thy money's worth for any goods thou mayst purchase. Master Mead bringeth good judgment to bear on his purchases, and buys only such goods as those in which he has confidence. Enter, friend; enter, I pray thee."

"Thank you," said Christison; "but I wish to see Master Mead himself."

"If thou wilt enter through this door, thou wilt find him in the upper story with his family," answered the shopman, leading the way; and Christison and Wenlock proceeded upstairs.

Master Mead cordially welcomed his old friend, introducing him to a comely matron whom he spoke of as his wife Martha. "And here is my daughter Mary," he added, pointing to a remarkably pretty and fair-haired girl, who smiled sweetly, and held out her hand to her father's guests. She might have been two or three years younger than Wenlock, though, being well grown, there seemed but little difference in their ages. While their elders were talking, the young people, after a few desultory remarks, found themselves drawn into conversation.

"I hear from my father that thou hast been a great traveller already," said Mary Mead.

"Yes, indeed," answered Wenlock. "I scarcely remember ever remaining more than two or three months in one place. When my mother died, my father left our home in New England, ever after seeking for some spot where he might settle, but finding none, till at length he determined to go back to the old country."

"You can have had but little time for obtaining instruction then?" said Mary, "I thought boys were always sent to school."

"I picked up what I could out of what my father calls the 'big book of life,'" answered Wenlock. "He also gave me such instructions as time and opportunity would allow, though there are many more things I should like to learn. I have, however, read not a few books; I can handle a singlestick as well as many older men, can ride, row, and shoot with arquebuse or crossbow, and I can write letters on various subjects, as I will prove to you, Mistress Mary, if you will allow me, when I again begin my wanderings; for I doubt whether my father will long remain in this big city. He is constantly complaining that the times are out of joint; and although we have been in England but a few weeks, he threatens again speedily to leave it."

"That were a pity," said Mary. "I prefer the green fields, and the woods, and the gay flowers, and the songs of birds, to the narrow streets, the dingy houses, and the cries of London; but yet I opine that happiness comes from within, and that, if the heart is at rest, contentment may be found under all circumstances."

"You are a philosopher," said Wenlock.

"No," answered Mary quietly, "I am a Quakeress, an you please: and our principles afford us that peace and contentment which they of the world know not of."

"I must get you to teach me to be a Quaker, then," said Wenlock. "I have been listening attentively to your father's discourses to mine, and even he, who was so much opposed to such ideas, has greatly been attracted by them; and, to tell you the truth, Mistress Mead, I have made up my mind that they are the best that I have heard of. There may be better, but I know not of them."

"Oh, no, no. There can be no better than such as are to be found in the Book of Life," said Mary. "You must judge of our principles by that, and that alone. If they are not according to that, they are wrong; but if they are according to that, there can be none better."

Wenlock, as he talked to the fair young Quakeress, felt himself every moment becoming more and more a convert to her opinions; and had not his father been present, he would then and there have undoubtedly confessed himself a Quaker.

The young people had found their way, somehow or other, to the bow window at the further end of the room, their elders, meantime, carrying on a conversation by themselves, not altogether of a different character. Mead, aided by his wife, was explaining to Christison, more fully than he had hitherto done, the Quaker doctrines. Could he, a man of the sword, however, acknowledge fighting to be wrong, and henceforth and for ever lay aside the weapons he had handled all his life?

"But surely, friend, if thou dost acknowledge that man is formed in God's image, it must be obvious to thee that to deface His image must be contrary to His law and will. The world is large, and God intends it to be peopled; whereas, by wars, the population ceases to increase, and that happy time when hymns of praise shall ascend from all quarters of the globe is postponed."

Mistress Mead occasionally made some telling remark to the same effect.

"Well, friend Mead, I have listened to all you have advanced," said Christison at length, "and I cannot, as an honest man, fail to acknowledge that you are in the main right. When next I come, I will hear what further arguments you have to adduce; but the truth is, when I determined to return to England, it was with the purpose of taking service in the English army, or in that of some foreign Protestant State, in which I hoped also to obtain employment for my son; whereas, if I turn Quaker, I must, I see, from what you tell me, give up all such ideas, and then how to obtain employment for him or myself I know not. I have no wish to be idle, and as 'a rolling stone gains no moss,' I have laid by but little of this world's wealth for a rainy day, or for my old age."

"Verily, thou must indeed give up all ideas of fighting and blood-shedding," answered Mead. "Yet I see not that thou needst starve. There is no lack of honest employments, if a man will but seek them. 'Thou canst not serve two masters.' Our God is a God of peace. The devil is the god of war; and devilish work is fighting, as I can answer from experience, and so canst thou, old comrade."

Christison sighed. "Well, well, friend," he said, "I feel you are right, and I will think over the matter. And now it is time that I should bid thee farewell. I have a visit to pay to a friend who lives some way on the other side of Temple Bar, and it will be late before we can get back to our lodgings."

Mead did not attempt to detain his friend. The young people started when Wenlock was summoned. They were sorry the visit had so soon come to an end.

"We shall see you again," said Mary, frankly putting out her hand, "and then I will speak to you more of these matters."

Wenlock of course promised that he would very soon come again. Christison and his son took their way along Cheapside, past old Saint Paul's, and proceeded down Ludgate Hill.

"You seemed pleased with young Mistress Mead, Wenlock," said his father.

"Come on, Wenlock," shouted the captain, rushing on.

"Indeed I was," answered Wenlock. "Though so quiet in manner, she has plenty to say. I never felt more inclined to talk in my life. I have promised to pay another visit as soon as I can, and when we go away, to write to her and give her an account of our adventures."

"You seem to have made progress in her good graces, Wenlock," said his father; and as he was a man of the world, it might possibly have occurred to him that when his son should desire a helpmate, fair Mistress Mary might prove a very suitable person. That perfect confidence existed between father and son which induced Wenlock to speak his mind on all occasions and on all subjects. They at length reached their destination, and the old soldier found his friend Lawrence Hargrave at home. In their conversation, which was chiefly on matters political, Wenlock took but little interest, his thoughts indeed being just then occupied chiefly by Mary Mead. He was glad, therefore, when his father announced his intention of returning home. They walked on rapidly, for the night was cold. It was dark also, for the sky was overcast. As they were going along Fleet Street, they heard the sound of horses' hoofs approaching at a somewhat rapid rate. They drew on one side, when a faint cry of "Help! help!" reached their ears.

"Come on, Wenlock," shouted the captain, rushing on. Directly before them they saw the outlines of two horses and several persons apparently struggling on the ground. The sounds of "Help! help!" again reached their ears.

"Here is help to whoever is in the right," cried Christison, drawing his sword.

"I am in the right; the others wish to kill me," said the same voice.

"No, no; he is a prisoner escaping from justice," growled a man in a rough voice.

"It is false! Help! I am the Duke—"

At that moment, a blow was heard, and the speaker was felled to the ground.

"I take the weakest side," cried Christison, attacking the other men, who now, drawing their swords, attempted to defend themselves. The old officer, a dextrous swordsman, disarmed the first, sending his weapon flying to the other side of the street. The next he attacked, giving him a severe wound on the arm. Young Wenlock, who, according to the fashion of the times, also wore a sword, joined in the fray, and made so furious an onset on the third fellow, who was at that moment about to run his weapon into the body of the prostrate man, that he compelled him to draw back. Placing himself across the body, he kept the fellow at bay, till another wound which his father bestowed on his antagonist made him retreat; when, the sound of carriage-wheels being heard in the distance, the three fellows, leaping on their horses, took to flight, leaving Christison and Wenlock masters of the field; the fallen man, only slightly stunned, had been slowly recovering; and when Christison stooped down to help him up, he was able, without much difficulty, to rise to his feet.

"Thanks, my friends, whoever you are," he said. "I observed the brave way in which you attacked my dastardly assailants; and I observed also the gallant manner in which this young gentleman defended me, when one of them would have run me through the body. To him I feel, indeed, that I am indebted for my life."

Chapter Six.

In a country house near Wanstead, in Essex, one of England's bravest admirals, — Sir William Penn, — lay on a bed of sickness. By his side stood a grave-looking gentleman in a scarlet cloak, and huge ruffles on his wrists.

"Tell me honestly, Master Kennard, whether you deem this sickness unto death?"

"Honestly, Sir William, as you ask me, I confess that you are in a worse state than I have before known you. At all events, it behoves you to make such preparations as you deem important, should you be summoned from the world."

"It is enough; I understand you, my friend," said the admiral, with a smile. "I would rather it were so. I am weary of the world, and am ready to leave it; but there is one who seems but little able to watch over his own interests, and, I fear me much, will be subjected to many persecutions in consequence of the opinions he has of late adopted. I would therefore ask you to indite a letter in my name to our gracious Sovereign and his royal brother, that I may petition them to extend to him those kind offices which they have ever shown to me. The Duke of York is his godfather, as you know; and, whatever may be his faults, he is an honest man, and will fulfil his promises. You will find paper and pen on yonder table. I pray thee perform this kind office for me."

Dr Kennard did as he was requested, and forthwith the letter was despatched by a trusty hand to London. Soon after it had been sent off, a servant announced that Master William Penn had just arrived, and craved permission to see his father. Grief was depicted on the countenance of the young man when he entered his father's chamber. He had just had an interview with his mother, and she had told him that all hopes of the admiral's recovery had been abandoned by his medical attendants. He knew not how his father might receive him. Although, when they last parted, the admiral's feelings had been somewhat softened towards his son, yet he had not even then ceased to blame him for the course he had pursued. Sir William Penn had already received numerous rewards and honours for the services he had rendered to his sovereign, and he had every reason to believe that he would have been raised to the peerage. His son William had, however, refused to accept any title, and he had therefore declined the honour for himself. He was now, however, at the early age of forty-nine, struck by a mortal disease, and he had begun to estimate more truly than heretofore the real value of wealth and worldly honours.

When William entered, he put out his hand.

"I thank Heaven, son William, you have come back to see me ere I quit this troubled scene of life," said the dying admiral. "I once wished to know that my son was to become a peer of the realm, the founder of a great family; but such thoughts have passed away from me. I now confess, William, that you have 'chosen the better part.' Your honour and glory no man can take away from you. In truth, I am weary of this world, and, had I my choice, would not live my days over again, for the snares of life are greater than the fears of death."

The affectionate son expressed his joy at hearing his father speak thus. The admiral smiled.

"Yes," he said, "our thoughts change when we see the portals of death so close to us. With regard to you, William, I am satisfied; but for our unhappy country I cannot cease to mourn. Alas! what fearful profligacy do we see in high places: vice and immorality rampant among all classes; the disrepute into which the monarchy and all connected with it have justly fallen; and the discredit into which our national character has been brought abroad."

William almost wept tears of joy when he described his father's state of mind to his mother. They could now converse freely on important matters. One day, while his son was with the admiral, two letters were brought him.

"Here," he said, "read them, son William, for my eyes are dim."

The young man took the letters.

"Indeed, father, they are such as should satisfy us," he said. "This one is from the king, who seldom puts pen to paper. He promises largely to protect me from all foes, and to watch over my interests. He expresses great regret at hearing of your illness, and wishes for your recovery. The other, from the Duke of York, is to the same effect. He speaks of his friendship to you for many years; and his sincere desire is, to render you all the service in his power. Therefore, with much satisfaction he undertakes the office of my guardian and protector when I am deprived of you. There is a kind tone throughout the epistle, for which I am duly grateful."

William then read both documents to his father, who desired to hear them. Still the admiral's constitution was good, and hopes were entertained that he might recover.

"My children," he said, calling his son and daughters to his bedside, "I have but a few days to live,—I know it. I leave you some worldly wealth, but that may be taken from you. I would leave you my counsel, of which no man can deprive you. There are three rules I would give you, which, if you follow them, will carry you with firmness and comfort through this inconstant world. Now listen to me. Let nothing in this world tempt you to wrong your conscience; so you will keep peace at home, which will be a feast to you in the day of trouble. Secondly, whatever you design to do, lay it justly, and time it seasonably, for that gives security and despatch. Lastly, be not troubled at disappointments, for if they may be recovered, do it; if they cannot, trouble is vain. If you could not have helped it, be content. There is often peace and profit in submitting to Providence; for afflictions make wise. If you could have helped it, let not your trouble exceed your instruction, for another time."

These rules, the admiral's son laid to heart; and, as his after life showed, they were never forgotten. William was greatly rewarded for all he had gone through by hearing his father at length thoroughly approve of his conduct.

"My son, I confess I would rather have you as you are, than among those frivolous and heartless courtiers who beset our sovereign. Their fate must be miserable. They are bringing reproach and ruin upon our country; and albeit, though I wish to die as I have lived, a member of the Church of England, yet I am well-content that you, my son, should be guided by the principles you have adopted; and I feel sure that if you and your friends keep to your plain way of preaching, and also keep to your plain way of living, you will make an end of priests to the end of the world." Almost the last words the admiral uttered were: "Bury me near my mother. Live all in love. Shun all manner of evil. I pray God to bless you; and He will bless you."

The spirit in which the admiral died, greatly softened the poignancy of the grief felt by his wife and son. The funeral procession set forth towards Bristol, where the admiral had desired to be buried, in Redcliffe Church, where a monument, still to be seen, was raised to his memory. William Penn was now the possessor of a handsome fortune inherited from his father. With youth, a fine appearance, fascinating manners, well acquainted with the world, numerous friends at court, and royal guardians pledged to advance his interests, he, notwithstanding, resisted all the allurements which these advantages offered to him, and set forth through the country, travelling from city to city, and village to village, preaching the simple gospel of salvation.

In a picturesque village in Buckinghamshire, called Chalfont, a young gentleman on horseback might have been seen passing up the chief street. There were but few people moving about at that early time of the morning. At length he saw one advancing towards him, who, though dressed in sober costume, had the air of a gentleman.

"Friend," said the young horseman, "canst tell me the abode of Master Isaac Pennington?"

William Penn on his way to the Grange, Chalfont.

"Ay! verily I can," answered the pedestrian; "and, if I mistake not, he to whom I speak is one who will be heartily welcome. His fame has gone before him in this region, remote as it is from the turmoils of the world. Thou art William Penn; I am Thomas Elwood, a friend of the family. Their abode is the Grange, which they have rebuilt and beautified. Further on, at the end of the street, is the dwelling of one known to all lovers of literature,—John Milton. And here is my cottage, where thou wilt be always welcome."

"Thanks, friend Elwood," said William Penn, dismounting from his horse. "If thou wilt show me the Grange, I will thank thee, and accept at another time thy hospitality."

"I am bound thither myself," said Elwood, "and I shall enjoy thy society on the way."

On reaching the Grange, William Penn found assembled in the breakfast parlour several guests. The lady of the house was Lady Springett, the widow of a Parliamentary officer; she had some years before married Isaac Pennington, both having adopted the Quaker principles. But there was one person present who seemed more especially to attract the young Quaker's attention. She was the daughter of Lady Springett; her name, Gulielma Maria, though addressed always by her family as Guli. William Penn had not been dreaming of love, but he at once felt himself drawn towards her; and before he left the Grange he acknowledged to himself that she had the power of adding greatly to his worldly happiness. Again, however, he went forth on his mission, but he frequently returned to Chalfont, and at length the fair Guli promised to become his wife.

Chapter Seven.

We left Captain Christison and his son just as they had gallantly rescued the stranger who had been set upon by ruffians in one of the principal thoroughfares of London. They had scarcely time to proceed far with him before they met a carriage accompanied by a couple of running footmen.

"O my lord duke! Are you safe? are you safe?" exclaimed the men.

"No thanks to your bravery, varlets," answered the nobleman. "Had it not been for these gentlemen, you would probably have never seen me again alive. And now, gentlemen," he said, turning to the captain and his son, "let me beg you will take a seat in my carriage, that I may convey you to your abode; or, if you will, honour me by coming to my mansion, that I may thank you more particularly for the essential service you have rendered me. I am the Duke of Ormonde. I was seated in my carriage, not dreaming of an attack, when two men suddenly opened the door, dragged me out, and, before my attendants could interfere, one of them, a powerful fellow, hoisted me up on the saddle before him. I struggled, and had just succeeded in bringing him with myself to the ground, when you came up. Why I have been thus assaulted I cannot tell, but I fear that it was in consequence of the animosity of some political opponents."

"Thank you, my lord duke," answered Christison. "We are lodging in the City, and I would not wish to take your grace so far out of your way, nor can we intrude upon you at this hour of the evening; but to-morrow morning we will, with your leave, wait on your grace. We have met before, though perhaps the recollection of the circumstances may not be altogether pleasant. I will not therefore now speak of them, though, as your grace at present sits on the upper end of the seesaw, you may look back on those days without annoyance."

"As you will," said the duke; "but you have not given me your name, and I should wish to recollect one who has rendered me so essential a service."

"Wenlock Christison,—an old soldier, an it please your grace," said the captain, introducing his son at the same time.

"Ah! ah! now I recollect you well, Captain Christison," answered the duke, "and truly I bear you no grudge because you sided with those I considered my foes; but let bygones be bygones, and I shall be very glad to see you again."

Saying this, with the help of his attendants, the duke entered his carriage, shaking hands very warmly with Wenlock. "I owe you a heavy debt, young gentleman," he said, "and one I shall at all times be glad to repay, and yet consider that I have not paid you sufficiently."

"A fortunate meeting," said Captain Christison to his son, as they walked on together. "The Duke of Ormonde is a powerful nobleman, and a truly upright and honest gentleman at the same time. What he promises he will fulfil. It is more than can be said of most of those in King Charles's court. Take my advice, Wenlock. Do not let this opportunity of gaining a good position in the world pass by. I do not suppose that he will offer me anything, but if he does, I shall be inclined to accept it. You see, Wenlock, our finances are far from being in a flourishing condition. I cannot turn to trade like my friend Mead, as I have no knowledge of it. In truth, as our family have always followed the calling of arms, or one of the liberal professions, I am not much disposed to yield to my worthy friend's arguments, and sheathe my sword for ever. I cannot understand why people should not be soldiers, and at the same time honest men and Christians."

"I will have a talk with Mistress Mary Mead on the subject," answered Wenlock, "when next we meet. At the same time I desire to follow your wishes, father."

"I rather suspect that Mistress Mary's bright eyes will weigh somewhat in the balance with her arguments, Master Wenlock," said his father, with a laugh. "However, we will pay our visit to the duke, and if he throws fortune in our way, I see not why we should refuse to clutch it."

The next morning was bright and dry. The captain and his son set off to pay their intended visit to the Duke of Ormonde. Wenlock, in his new slash doublet and hose, with a feather in his cap and a sword by his side, looked a brave young gallant, as in truth he was.

His father gazed at him proudly. "It were a pity," thought the old soldier to himself, "to see the lad turn Quaker, and throw away the brilliant prospects he has of rising in the world. Such a chance as this may never occur to him again; for though I perchance might get him a commission in a troop of horse with myself, yet he would have many hard blows to strike before he could rise to fortune and fame, while a bullet might, long ere he reached them, cut short his career."

On arriving at the Duke of Ormonde's residence, they were at once shown into an ante-chamber, where two or three pages in attendance minutely scrutinised young Wenlock. They suspected, perhaps, from his manner and appearance, that he had come to take service with them. Courtesy, however, prevented them making any inquiries on the subject. After a short time, a gentleman came out of the duke's chamber and invited Captain Christison and his son to enter. His manner was especially respectful, and this evidently raised the visitors in the opinion of the young pages. The duke came forward and shook Captain Christison cordially by the hand. He received Wenlock in a still more kind manner. Then turning to a dignified young man by his side, he said, "Allow me to introduce you to my son Ossory. He desires also to thank you for the service you have rendered his father."

"Indeed I do, gentlemen," said Lord Ossory, coming forward; "and I only hope that this young gentleman will allow me to show my gratitude. Who the villains were from whom you rescued the duke we have been as yet unable to ascertain, but there can be no doubt that their purpose was to murder him; indeed, preparations for hanging some one were found made this morning under the gibbet at Tyburn; and coupling this with a threatening letter received a few days ago by the duke, we suspect that they intended to put him thus ignominiously to death."

Captain Christison made a suitable reply to these remarks of the duke and the earl. "As to myself," he said, "I have been a stranger to England for many years, and came home for the sake of seeing my native land again, and then taking service afloat or on shore, wherever I might find my sword acceptable, and my conscience would allow me."

"I understand you, my friend," said the duke; "and since old foes have shaken hands, and Roundheads and Cavaliers now unite together, I trust that you will not object to accept a company in my regiment. As senior captain, you will have the command; and as you have fought at sea, you will not object, I presume, to serve again on board ship, should a war break out. Lord Ossory, who is in the navy, desires to retain your son about his own person, should the young gentleman like to see something of the world. Otherwise, I should be glad to give him a post in my household."

"You overwhelm us with kindnesses, my lord duke," said Captain Christison. "For myself, nothing would suit me better than what you propose, and I must beg to leave my son to choose for himself. What say you, Wenlock? Do you wish to take time to think on the matter, or will you run the chance of seeing service under the noble Earl of Ossory?"

The worldly ambition of the old soldier, excited by the flattering remarks of the duke, imparted itself to Wenlock. Could he make up his mind to turn draper's assistant in the City, as he had been meditating doing yesterday, while so brilliant a prospect had opened itself up before him? The thought were ridiculous.

"I heartily accept the offer of the Earl of Ossory, my lord duke," he said, with a bow which could not have been surpassed had he been all his life at court. "I could not wish to serve under a more noble and gallant leader."

"I am glad it is so settled," said the Duke. "To be frank with you, Captain Christison, I remember you well, and the good service you did to the cause you advocated. I have not forgotten, either, the courteous way in which you treated me when I fell into your hands on the fatal field of Worcester; and, by my troth, the way the Cavaliers behaved on that occasion made me ashamed of my order and the cause I served. You tell me that you are lodging in the City. You can, however, move here as soon as you please. There are rooms for you both, and places at my table. In truth, after the dastardly attack made upon me last night, I shall be thankful to have two such trusty friends within call, for I know not when I may be again assaulted."

Thus invited, the captain and his son were glad to move that very evening to the duke's house; indeed, the few gold pieces remaining in the old soldier's purse reminded him that he must find some speedy means of replenishing it, or run the risk of having to live upon short commons. The captain had never been a prudent man, and Wenlock little thought what a hole the cost of his suit had made in his father's exchequer.

Chapter Eight.

"And thou art going away on board a warship to fight and slay, and, alack! perchance to be slain," said Mary Mead, whose hand was held by Wenlock Christison. "It is sad to think of such cruel deeds, and sadder still that thou, Wenlock, should engage in such work. I had thought my father had shown thee the sinfulness of warfare, and that I might have said something to the same effect that might have moved thee."

"So you did, Mary; and when I am with you truly I feel inclined to play the woman, and, throwing up all my brilliant prospects, to join myself to your father or Master William Penn, and to go forth as they are wont to do to promulgate their doctrines."

"Nay; but that would not be playing the woman, surely," said Mary, reproachfully. "It is no woman's work they have to go through, although some women are found who boldly go forth even into foreign lands, and, in spite of danger and opposition, are not behind the men in zeal in the good cause."

"I am wrong, Mary, thus to speak. I should greatly have disappointed my father had I refused to serve under the Earl of Ossory; besides which, no other means are open to me of supporting myself. I must, I find, depend upon my sword; for my father now tells me, what I did not before know, that all his means are expended, and that without a profession I should be little better than a beggar."

"Alack! alack!" said poor Mary, and the tears came into her eyes. "For 'they that take the sword shall perish with the sword.' You know, Wenlock, too, that my father would gladly have found employment for you, if you would have accepted it."

This remark came home to Wenlock's heart. It was the truth, and he could not help acknowledging that he had preferred his worldly associates, and the so-called brilliant prospects offered to him by the earl, instead of becoming a haberdasher's apprentice, an humble Quaker, and the husband of the pretty Mary Mead. He still hoped, indeed, to win her. She had acknowledged her love for him, and he had built up many castles in the air of which she was to be the mistress. After serving a few years under Lord Ossory, he expected to rise in rank, and to come home with ample wealth, which would enable him to settle down on shore, and marry her. Master Mead had parted from Captain Christison somewhat coldly. He bade Wenlock farewell with a sigh.

"Thou hast been led to act as thou art doing by thy father, and I cannot blame thee," he said. "I had hoped better things of thee, and I would now pray that thy heart may be turned to the right way."

Mary was very sad after Wenlock had gone. He was frank and artless, good-looking, and of agreeable manners; and believing that he was about to join her sect, she had given her heart to him without reserve. He had come frequently to the house after he had taken service under Lord Ossory, though his duties had of late prevented his visits being as frequent as at first. Several months had thus passed away, his father having in the meantime joined the fleet under the Earl of Sandwich, one of the bravest of England's admirals at that time. He would have taken Wenlock with him, had not Lord Ossory desired that the young man should remain in his service. The morning after parting from Mary, Wenlock accompanied Lord Ossory to Portsmouth. Here a ship of sixty guns, the *Resolution*, was waiting to receive the earl as her captain.

Not till Wenlock was on board, and sailing out from Spithead past Saint Helen's, had he any notion whither the fleet was bound. He, with several other young men and boys, were occupants of part of the captain's cabin, which was devoted to them.

"You will see some service, Christison," said the earl. "I wish it were of a more worthy character than it is likely to prove. King Charles's exchequer is low, and we have been sent out here to capture a homeward-bound fleet of Dutch merchantmen expected shortly in the Channel. You heard the other day of the Dutch refusing to strike their flag when the *Merlin* yacht passed through their fleet with Lady Temple on board. Her captain fired in return, and was rewarded with a gold chain on his arrival at home. This is our pretence, a sorry one, I confess, for war."

The *Resolution* formed one of the fleet under Sir Robert Holmes, consisting altogether of some thirty-six men-of-war. Eight only had, however, been got ready for sea, and with these Sir Robert was about to take a short cruise outside the Isle of Wight, for practising the crews. Scarcely, however, had they lost sight of land before the *Resolution*, being to the westward, descried a fleet standing up Channel. She communicated the intelligence to the rest of the squadron. They were soon made out to be Dutch. The sea officers, after examining them carefully, declared that there were several men-of-war among them. On their approaching nearer, of this there was no doubt. Sir Robert Holmes, however, followed by the *Resolution*, stood gallantly towards them, when in addition to the seventy merchantmen expected, six stout men-of-war were perceived. Of the English ships five were frigates. The Dutch, who had timely notice of the intended attack, were prepared for battle, with their decks cleared, divided into three squadrons, each guarded by two men-of-war, and together forming a half-moon. Sir Robert approaching them, ordered them to strike their flags. On their refusing to do so, he fired a broadside into the nearest ship. They, however, lowered their topsails. Again he asked whether they would strike their flags. On their refusing, he again fired; and now the action became general.

Sir Robert especially attacked the ship of the Dutch commodore, while Lord Ossory attacked another commanded by Captain du Bois. For some hours the action continued, but so well did the Dutch defend themselves, that when darkness put an end to the fight, no material advantage had been gained. The next day, however, the English fleet being joined by four more frigates from Portsmouth, again attacked the Dutch. Lord Ossory gallantly boarded Captain du Bois' ship. Wenlock was among the first to dash on to the deck of the enemy. His swordsmanship served him in good stead. Many, however, of his companions were killed around him, and for some time he was left with but few followers on the enemy's deck. Lord Ossory, seeing the danger of his young officer, calling upon his men, led a fresh body of boarder on to the deck of the enemy. In spite however of his valour, they were driven back on board his own ship. Out of the whole Dutch squadron, indeed, when darkness again came on, only one man-of-war and three merchantmen had been captured. With these Sir Robert was compelled to return to port, the Dutchmen making good their escape.

"It was scurvy work," exclaimed Lord Ossory, as the ship came to an anchor. "Such is unfit for gallant gentlemen to engage in. I would rather sheathe my sword, and forswear fighting for the future, than to undertake again such a buccaneering business."

Wenlock, however, had got a taste for sea life. His gallantry in the action had been remarked, and was highly commended. When therefore the *Royal James*, on board which his father was serving under the Earl of Sandwich, came to an anchor, he begged that he also might join her. Through Lord Ossory's introduction, the admiral received him very courteously, and promised to look after his interests. The captain of the ship, Sir Richard Haddock, also expressed his satisfaction at having him on board.

The *Royal James* was one of the largest ships in the navy, carrying a hundred guns, and nearly one thousand men, including seamen and soldiers. Captain Christison, now in his element, was delighted to have his son with him, and well-pleased at the credit the young man had gained.

"You will see some real fighting before long, Wenlock," he observed. "Braver men than Lord Sandwich and his captain do not exist, and now this war with the Dutch has broken out we shall not let their fleets alone."

Some time after this, the English fleets, consisting of nearly a hundred sail, under the command of the Duke of York, the Earl of Sandwich being the admiral of the blue squadron, were lying at Spithead. War had been declared against the Dutch, in reality at the instigation of France, whose armies were at the same time pouring into Holland. Early in May, a French fleet of forty-eight ships, under the command of Count d'Estrees, arrived at Portsmouth, and soon afterwards he and the English together put to sea. After cruising about for some time in search of the enemy, they anchored in Sole Bay.

"Wenlock, before many days are over you will have seen a real sea-fight. The very thought of it warms up my old blood," exclaimed his father. "I know you will acquit yourself well; and if the enemy's fleet falls into our hands, as I doubt not it will, we shall have no cause henceforth to complain of want of money in our purses."

Alas! what would Mary Mead, what would her father and William Penn, have said to such sentiments?

Chapter Nine.

The English and French fleets lay in Sole Bay, a brave sight, with flags flying and trumpets sounding from the different ships. Just as day broke on the 28th of May, numerous sail were seen dotting the horizon. On they came. There was no doubt that they were the ships of the Dutch fleet. The Duke of York threw out the signal for action; and the ships setting sail, some of them cutting their cables in their eagerness, stood out of the bay. The French, who were on the outside, were nearest to the Dutch. From the deck of the *Royal James*, no less than seventy-five large ships were discovered, and forty frigates. The fleet was commanded, as was well known, by the brave Admirals de Ruyter, Banquert, and Van Ghent. The French were first attacked by Admiral Banquert. And now the guns on both sides sent forth their missiles of death,—round shot and chain shot, the latter cutting to pieces the rigging and spars of their antagonists.

"See, Wenlock, those Frenchmen fight well," exclaimed Christison. "We must acquit ourselves in a like gallant way." This was said as the *Royal James* was standing into action, approaching a large Dutch ship called the *Great Holland*. "But see! what are they about? They are beating a retreat. Two or three of their ships remain in the enemy's hands. They have no stomach for the fight, that is clear; or, from what I hear, they are playing the game they have long done. It is the old story. They wish the Dutch and us to tear ourselves to pieces, and then they will come in and pick up the fragments."

Meantime, the Duke of York in the *Saint Michael* was engaged with Admiral de Ruyter, his ship being so severely handled that he had to leave her, and hoist his flag on board the *Loyal London*.

"Ah! we have enemies enough coming down upon us," exclaimed Christison, as the *Royal James*, at the head of the blue squadron, became almost surrounded by Dutch ships. The *Great Holland* was the first to lay her alongside, the Dutchmen, however, in vain endeavouring to board. Admiral Van Ghent next attacked her with a squadron of fire-ships. The brave Earl of Sandwich encouraged his men to resist, in spite of the numerous foes round him. Again and again the Dutchmen from the deck of the *Great Holland* attempted to carry the *Royal James*. Each time they were beaten back. Sometimes the earl put himself at the head of his men; at others Christison and his son repelling the boarders. All this time the other Dutch ships kept up a terrific fire on the *Royal James*. More than once the earl turned his eyes towards the remainder of the English fleet, but none of the ships seemed prepared to come to his assistance. The Englishmen were falling thickly; already many hundreds strewed the deck.

"When a man's destruction has been resolved on, it is easy to bring it about," observed the earl to his captain, Sir Richard Haddock, who stood by his side. "However, neither friends nor foes shall say that Edward Montagu failed in his duty to his country, or ceased to fight till the last." Saying this, he again cheered his men. Never did a crew fight with more fierce desperation than did that of the *Royal James*. Even the wounded refused to quit their guns, till they dropped at their quarters. A cheer at length arose from their decks. The *Great Holland* had been beaten off, and was retiring in a disabled state. De Ruyter, his person conspicuous on the deck of his ship, still assailed her however. At length a shot was seen to strike him, and he sank, apparently slain, to the deck.

For a short time the hard-pressed ship of the gallant admiral enjoyed a respite; but by this time she was reduced almost to a wreck, while six hundred of her brave crew lay dead or dying about her decks, with many of her officers, and several gallant gentlemen who had volunteered on board. Night was coming on, the constant flashes from the guns, however, showing the fury with which the fight was continued. Still the earl refused to retire from the combat. Christison and his son had hitherto escaped. "I have seen many fierce battles, Wenlock, but never one like this," said the old officer; "and our fighting is not over to-day. See here come more foes!" As he spoke, several ships were seen bearing down upon the *Royal James*, and now, opening their fire, they surrounded her with smoke. The four hundred survivors of her crew fought their guns with the same desperation as at first; but in the midst of the smoke a ship, approaching unperceived, grappled closely with her. Directly afterwards there was a cry of fire!

Flames were seen bursting forth from the enemy, now, when too late, known to be a fire-ship. In vain the crew endeavoured to free themselves from her, but the Dutch sent such showers of shot among them that many were killed in the attempt. Wenlock had been keeping near his father, who, for the first time since the commencement of the fight, acknowledged that they were in desperate circumstances. Scarcely had he spoken, when Wenlock heard a sharp cry by his side, and turning round, he saw his father falling to the deck. He lifted him up; but as he gazed in his countenance, he saw that those eyes which had always looked at him with affection were glazing in death.

"Father! father! speak to me," said Wenlock; but there was no answer. He laid him down on the deck. And now on every side the flames were bursting forth through the ports. Already the fore part of the ship was a mass of fire. Just then the brave Sir Richard Haddock received a shot in the thigh. He fell, but again raised himself to his feet: "Lower the boats, lads!" he shouted. "Ere a few minutes are over, no one will be able to live on board our stout ship. Where is the earl?"

"He went to his cabin," answered some one.

"Christison, come with me; we must get him into a boat. I fear he is wounded." Wenlock was obeying his commander, when just at that moment he felt a severe pang, and was conscious that a missile of some sort had passed through his side. In spite of his wound, however, he followed the captain. The earl was seated at the table, with a handkerchief over his eyes.

"My lord, a boat is in readiness, and we have come to conduct you to it," said Sir Richard.

"No, friend, no," answered the earl. "I cannot brook some bitter words spoken to me yesterday by the Duke of York. If my ship is to perish, I will perish with her."

In vain Sir Richard and Wenlock tried to persuade the brave earl to listen to reason. Already the crackling sounds of the flames were heard, and wreaths of smoke came driving into the cabin. Then came a terrific sound. Wenlock scarcely knew what had happened, when he found himself plunged into the water. He was a strong swimmer, and struck out for life. Near him was another man whose features, lighted up by the flames from the burning ship, he recognised as those of Sir Richard Haddock. He swam towards him.

"Leave me, Christison," he said; "I am desperately wounded, and cannot survive this night. You too I saw were wounded, and will have enough to do to save yourself."

"No, no, sir," answered Wenlock; "I see close to us a spar. It will support us till some help arrives. I will tow you towards it if you will float quietly."

Sir Richard did as he was advised, and in a short space of time Wenlock had placed him on the spar. It was not, however, sufficient to support both of them.

Another was seen at a little distance. Securing the captain to the first, Wenlock swam to the other. He had wished to remain by his captain, but by some means he perceived that they were gradually receding from each other. In vain he shouted to the ships nearest to him. The din of battle drowned his voice. First one tall ship, then another, went down. The whole ocean around seemed covered with fragments of wrecks and struggling men. Of the latter, one after the other, however, sunk below the surface. At length he saw several ships approaching him. Again he shouted. It seemed to him that one was about to run over him, and courageous as he was, he gave himself up for lost. Leaving the spar, he swam off, hoping thus to avoid her. She must have been hotly engaged, for her topmasts and all their rigging were hanging over the side. As the ship passed by, he caught hold of the rigging, and drawing himself up, found a firm footing. Though his wound pained him considerably, he still had sufficient strength to climb on board, not knowing as he did so whether he was to find himself among friends or foes.

Chapter Ten.

Almost exhausted, pale as death, the blood flowing from his wound opened by the exertions he had made, Wenlock Christison dropped down on the deck of the stranger, not knowing whether he was to find himself on board an English or Dutch ship. The condition of the ship showed that she had been hotly engaged, for numbers of dead men lay about her blood-stained decks. From their appearance, as the light of the lanterns occasionally glanced on them, Wenlock at once saw that they were Dutch. Dutch was among the languages with which he was acquainted, having met many Hollanders in America.

"Who are you?" said an officer, who saw him come over the side.

"An Englishman, and one of the few survivors of the ill-fated ship which blew up just now," he answered. "Well-nigh a thousand men who walked her decks in health and strength this morning are now in eternity."

"You are indeed fortunate in escaping then," said the Dutch officer, "and though we must consider you a prisoner, you will be treated with due courtesy on board this ship. I see that you are wounded, and badly it seems to me, so that you must be forthwith put under the surgeon's care."

Wenlock thanked him, and supported by a couple of men was carried below. After this he knew nothing of what happened to him, for scarcely had he been placed on a bed than he fainted. When he came to consciousness he found the surgeon ready to administer some medicine, soon after which he fell asleep, nor did he awake again till daylight. He inquired eagerly what had occurred.

"You must not talk much," said the surgeon; "but this I will tell you, that we have had a very fierce engagement, and lost three of our stoutest ships; while, if the truth is known, you English have not been less sufferers. Depend on it, altogether between us, four or five thousand people have been killed: a sensible employment for human beings. Heu! while we, —a free Protestant people, —were fighting for liberty, you English were beguiled by your own traitorous sovereign, bribed by the King of France, to attack us."

The surgeon, Nicholas Van Erk, notwithstanding his remarks, treated Wenlock with the greatest kindness. They however gave him ample material for thought. In a short time the Dutch fleet arrived off the coast of Holland, and the injured ships proceeded to the chief naval ports to undergo repair. The *Marten Harptez*, the ship on board which Wenlock had found refuge, proceeded to Rotterdam.

"You are a prisoner, but I have got leave to receive you at my house," said Mynheer Van Erk; "and as I have a good many sick men to look after, I do not purpose again going to sea. In truth, fighting may be a very satisfactory amusement to people without brains; but I am a philosopher, and have seen enough of it to be satisfied that it is a most detestable occupation."

Wenlock found himself conveyed to a comfortable mansion in Rotterdam overlooking a canal; indeed, what houses do not overlook canals in that city? He was very weak, for his wound had been severe, —more severe than he had supposed; and he was surprised that he should have been enabled to undergo so much exertion as he had done. Van Erk, indeed, told him that had he remained much longer in the water, he would probably have fainted from loss of blood, and been drowned.

"As you may become a wise man and enjoy life, being young, that would have been a pity," observed the philosopher; "but it depends how you spend the future whether you should or should not be justly congratulated on your escape."

The doctor's wife and only daughter, —the fair Frowline Gretchen, — formed the only members of the surgeon's household, with their serving maid Barbara. They, fortunately for Wenlock, were not philosophers, but turned their attention to household affairs, and watched over him with the greatest care. He, poor fellow, felt very sad and forlorn. For many days he could only think with deep grief of the untimely loss of his brave father. In time, however, he began to meditate a little also about himself. All his prospects appeared blighted. The friends who might have spoken of his brave conduct in the fight were dead. He had hoped to obtain wealth, and to return and marry Mary Mead. He had not a groat remaining in the world. Never in his life before had he been so downhearted Gretchen observed his melancholy.

"You should not thus grieve for being a prisoner," she observed; "many brave men have been so, and the time will come when you will be set at liberty."

Wenlock then told her how he had lost his father, and how his own hopes of advancement had been blighted. "Have you no one then who cares for you?" she asked, in a tone of sympathy; "no one in your native land to whom you desire to return?"

"Yes," said Wenlock; and he then told her of his engagement to the fair Quakeress.

"Ah! I am not surprised at that," observed the Dutch girl, with a sigh. After this, though as kind as usual, Wenlock observed that she was somewhat more distant in her manner to him than she had been at first.

Considering that he was a prisoner, his time passed very pleasantly. Having given his word to the authorities and to his host that he would not attempt to escape, he was allowed to go about that picturesque town as much as he pleased. Month after month the war continued, and he remained a prisoner. His affection, however, for Mary Mead had rather increased by absence than diminished; and fearing that she might forget him, he at length wrote her a letter, entreating her to remain faithful, and promising, as soon as he should be able, to return to England and follow any course she might advise. In vain he waited for an answer to this letter; week after week passed by, and none came.

"She has forgotten you," said Gretchen one day, observing him look very sad.

Wenlock started! He was thinking the same thing. "I know not," he answered; "I have heard that women are fickle."

"I did not say that," observed Gretchen; "but if you chose to disregard the wishes of one you professed to love, I am not surprised that she should at length have dismissed you from her thoughts. I do not say she has, but it is possible."

Wenlock had for some time felt ashamed of being idle; for though his host might have received payment for his support from the government, yet that, he was sure, could not be sufficient to cover the expense to which he was put. He expressed his wishes to his kind host.

"A very sensible remark," observed the surgeon, "and as you have now recovered from your wound, and regained your strength, it is proper that you should be employed. I have a brother, a merchant, trading with Surinam. He may possibly give you employment. You speak several languages, and write a good hand. You will, I doubt not, soon be ranked among his principal clerks, if you have a good knowledge of accounts."

"If he will try me, I will do my best," answered Wenlock.

The next day he was installed as a clerk in the office of Peter Van Erk, one of the principal merchants in the city. Wenlock had an aptitude for business of which he had not been aware. He took a positive pleasure in his work, and soon attracted the observation of his quick-sighted employer.

The kind surgeon was highly pleased. "You do credit to my recommendation, Christison," he observed; "you will soon win the confidence of my brother, and will then be on the fair way to making your fortune."

Time passed by. Wenlock made himself so useful that in a short time his employer agreed to pay him a handsome salary. When peace was declared, therefore, he felt that it would be folly to return to England, where he had no home and no one from whom he had a right to demand assistance. He had forfeited William Mead's regard by acting contrary to his advice, while from Lord Ossory he might possibly fail to receive further patronage. He had heard enough of the fickleness of those in authority, and he did not expect to be better treated than others. He therefore continued to work away steadily as a merchant's clerk in the house of Van Erk and Company, of Rotterdam.

Chapter Eleven.

"Come with my mother and me to a meeting to which we are going this evening!" said Gretchen, when Wenlock returned home at a somewhat earlier hour than usual, for he still lived at the house of the kind surgeon. "Some Englishmen arrived yesterday in Rotterdam, and they are about to address the public on some important religious matters. They are said to be very earnest and devoted people, and one of them speaks Dutch perfectly. Their names I cannot remember. Those short, curious, English names quickly escape my memory."

Wenlock at once agreed to Gretchen's request; indeed he had no longer the heart to refuse her anything she asked. It might have been just possible that, had he learned that the fair Mary had forgotten him and accepted another suitor, he would have had no great difficulty in consoling himself. Yet it was not so at present. He always treated Gretchen with kindness and respect, but was fully convinced in his own mind that he never allowed a warmer feeling to enter his bosom. The large public hall in which meetings of the sort were generally held was nearly filled by the time the Van Erk party arrived. They, however, were shown to seats near the platform whence the speakers were to address the people. Many more persons crowded in, till the hall was quite full. Just then five gentlemen appeared on the platform, advancing with slow and dignified steps. A curious and very mixed feeling agitated Wenlock's heart when among them he recognised Master William Penn, and his father's old friend, Captain Mead. The thought of his father rushed into his mind, and a tear filled his eye. He thought, however, also of Mary, and he longed to ask her father about her; yet, at that moment, to do so was impossible. As the speakers appeared, the whole hall was hushed in silence. At length William Penn offered up a prayer in Dutch. He then introduced a tall thin, careworn man, as George Fox, who addressed the people in English, Penn interpreting as he spoke. He urged on them in forcible language to adopt the principles which the Friends had accepted, and many were moved to tears while he spoke. William Mead then came forward, but said little. Another

Englishman, Robert Barclay, then addressed the assemblage. He was followed by Penn himself; who, in calm yet forcible language, placed the simple truths of the gospel before his hearers. Wenlock's feelings were greatly moved. His reason too was convinced. He had had a severe lesson. He had declined to accept those principles, and sought for worldly honour and distinction instead. The result had been the loss of his beloved father, he himself escaping with life almost by a miracle. "Those are old friends I little expected to meet again," said Wenlock to Gretchen and her mother. "I must speak to them now, lest they leave the city to-morrow and I may miss them."

As the assembly broke up, the speakers descended into the body of the hall, and Wenlock found himself standing before William Penn and Captain Mead. Neither of them knew him, though they looked at him kindly, having observed the deep attention with which he had listened to their discourses. "I am afraid, Master Mead, I am forgotten," said Wenlock, feeling that he must speak at last. The Quaker started, and examined his countenance narrowly. "What!" he exclaimed, "art thou the son of my ancient comrade? Verily I thought that he and thou were long since numbered with the dead. How is it, young man? Has thy father escaped also?"

"Alas! no," said Wenlock; and he gave a brief account of his father's death.

"And hast thou been content to pass so long a time without communicating with thy old friends?" said Mead, in a reproachful tone.

"No, indeed. I wrote to Mistress Mary," said Wenlock; "but she replied not to my letter."

"My daughter received no letter from thee, young man," said Mead; "and I will not deny that she grieved at the thought of thy loss."

"O Master Mead, I wish that I had written oftener, till one of my letters had reached you or her," exclaimed Wenlock; "but I thought that she had discarded me."

"I see; I see! And thou wast too proud to run the risk of being chid further for thy youthful folly," said the Quaker.

"You are right, I confess," answered Wenlock. "But tell me, how is she? Where is she? Would I could once more see her and explain my conduct."

"Perchance thou mayst see her sooner than thou dost expect," said Mead. "Come to-morrow morning to the house where we lodge, and we will talk further of this matter."

"What! is she in Rotterdam?" exclaimed Wenlock, in a voice trembling with agitation.

"She accompanied us thus far on our journey; but I know not whether she will go farther. I must not let thee see her, however, to-night, as, believing thee dead, it might perchance somewhat agitate her; for I do not deny, Wenlock, that thou wast once dear to us all. But whether thou canst sufficiently explain thy conduct since thou didst part from us, to regain thy lost place in our regard, I cannot now determine."

"Oh, I trust I can," exclaimed Wenlock, all his affection for Mary reviving immediately at the thought of again meeting her.

William Penn received the young man very kindly, and then for some minutes spoke to him with deep seriousness of his past life. "Thou canst not serve God and Mammon, Friend Wenlock," he said. "Thou didst attempt to do so, and Mammon left thee struggling for thy life on the ocean. More on that matter I need not say."

Wenlock, on reaching home, found that his friends had been deeply impressed by the addresses they had heard. They were also much surprised to find that two of the speakers were known to him.

"Indeed, one of them," he said, "is a very old friend; and should he invite me to accompany him to England, I should wish to do so."

"What! and leave us all here, not to return?" said Gretchen.

"It is right that I should tell the truth at once," thought Wenlock. He did so.

"And is this English girl very, very pretty," asked Gretchen; and her voice trembled slightly.

"I thought her so when we parted; and amiable, and right-minded, and pious I know she is."

"Ah!" said Gretchen, "I should like to see her while she remains in this city."

The next morning Wenlock set out to pay his promised visit to his Quaker friends. Master Mead met him at the door of the house.

"Come in; Mary will see thee," he said; and taking him upstairs, he led him into a room, at the farther end of which a young lady was seated with a book before her. She rose as her father and their visitor entered, and gave an inquiring glance at Wenlock, apparently at first scarcely knowing him. Another look assured her who it was, but no smile lighted up her countenance. She advanced, however, and held out her hand. "Thou art welcome, Master Christison," she said; "and I rejoice to find that thou didst escape the sad fate we heard had overtaken thee. And yet, was it kind to leave old friends who were interested in thee, albeit thou didst differ from them in opinion, without knowing of thy existence?" Her voice, which had hitherto remained firm, began to tremble.

"Oh, no, no, Mary!" exclaimed Wenlock. "I cannot blame myself too much. Yet I did write; but I ought to have written again and again, till I heard from you. I should have known that the risk of a letter miscarrying was very great."

"Yea; verily thou ought to have put more confidence in us," said Mary.

Then Wenlock again blamed himself, and Mary showed herself before long inclined to be more lenient than her manner had at first led him to hope she might prove.

Penn and his party remained for some days at Rotterdam, holding numerous meetings. Many among the most educated of the inhabitants,—officers of the government, merchants, and others,—came to hear them preach; while many of the principal houses of the place were thrown open to them. Among other converts was Wenlock's employer, Mynheer Van Erk, as was also his kind friend the surgeon and his family. Gretchen and Mary met frequently. "You have not over praised the English maiden," said the former to Wenlock. "I hope you will be fortunate in regaining her regard; for it is clear to me that you still look on her with affection."

Penn, with three of his companions, proceeded on their tour through Holland and part of Germany, gaining many proselytes to their opinions. Mead, who had some mercantile transactions at Rotterdam, remained in that city. After they were concluded he prepared to return home. Wenlock wished to accompany him. "No, my young friend," he answered, "I cannot allow thee to quit thy present employer without due notice. Should he wish to dispense with thy services, I will receive thee when thou dost come to me." Wenlock had now openly professed himself to be a Quaker. Perchance, Master Mead, who had no lack of worldly wisdom, desired to try the young man's constancy, both as to his love and his religion; for, in both, people are very apt to deceive themselves, mistaking enthusiasm and momentary excitement for well grounded principle. As winter approached, Penn and his party returned to Rotterdam, and sailed for England.

Chapter Twelve.

The beams of the evening sun were streaming through a deep bay window of the country house of Worminghurst, in Sussex, on the heads of two men seated at a large oak writing table in a room which, lined as it was with bookcases, showed that it was devoted to study.

The heads of both of them betokened high intellect, traces of care and thought being especially discernible on the countenance of the elder,—that lofty intellect to be quenched, ere a few short years were over, by the executioner's axe,—a deed as cruel and unjust as any caused by the cowardice and tyranny of a monarch.

The table was covered with parchments, papers, books, and writing materials. Both were holding pens in their hands, now and then making note from the documents before them, at other times stopping and addressing each other. The younger man was William Penn, who, lately having obtained a grant of a large tract of country on the American continent, was now engaged in drawing up a constitution for its government, assisted by the elder,—the enlightened patriot and philosopher, Sidney.

"See! such a constitution as this for Carolina will not suit a free people such as will be our colonists!" said the former, pointing to a document before him, "albeit it emanated from the brain of John Locke. Here we have a king, though with the title of palatine, with a whole court and two orders of nobility. Laws to prevent estates accumulating or diminishing. The children of leet men to be leet men for ever, while every free man is to have power over his negro slaves. Truly, society will thus be bound hand and foot. All political rights to be taken from the cultivators of the soil. Trial by jury virtually set aside. The Church of England to be alone the true and orthodox, and to be supported out of the coffers of the State."

"In truth, no," said Sidney. "John Locke has not emancipated himself from his admiration of the feudal system. Let this be our principle,—

that those whose lives, properties, and liberties are most concerned in the administration of the laws shall be the people to form them. Let there be two bodies to be elected by the people, — a council and an assembly. Let the council consist of seventy-two persons, to be chosen by universal suffrage, for three years, twenty-four of them retiring every year, their places to be supplied by new election. Let the members of the assembly be elected annually, and all votes taken by ballot. The suffrage to be universal. Let it have the privilege of making out the list of persons to be named as justices and sheriffs, and let the governor be bound to select one half of those thus recommended. Now we must consider numerous provisional laws relating to liberty of conscience, provision for the poor, choice of civil officers, and so on, which can be in force until accepted by the council. We shall thus, dear friend, I trust, have secured freedom of thought, the sacredness of person and property, popular control over all powers of the state; and we will leave our new democracy to develop itself in accordance with its own genius, unencumbered with useless formalities and laws."

"Yes; I trust that the simplicity of our constitution will secure its permanence," said Sidney. "I will take the papers home with me to Penshurst, and there maturely consider over all the points."

Left alone, William Penn might have been seen lifting up his hands in earnest prayer to heaven that his noble scheme might prosper. He was interrupted by a knock at the door, and a servant announced a visitor. In another minute a young man entered the room with modest air and in sober costume.

"Who art thou?" said Penn, looking up.

"Wenlock Christison," answered the visitor. "I came at the desire of Friend Mead."

"Yea; I wish to see thee, young friend," said Penn; "but when thou earnest into the room I did not at first recognise thee. Thou art somewhat changed, I may say, for the better. Sit down, and I will tell thee what I require. Look at this map of the American continent. See this magnificent river,—the Delaware, entering the Atlantic between Cape Henlopen and Cape May. See those other fine rivers,—the Susquehannah, the Ohio, and the Alleghany. Here is a country but a little less than the size of England; its surface covered with a rich vegetable loam capable of the highest cultivation, and of producing wheat, barley, rye, Indian corn, hemp, oats, flax. Here too are mighty forests supplying woods of every kind, abounding too in wild game and venison, equal to any in England. The rivers are full of fish, oysters, and crabs in abundance. On the coast the most luscious fruits grow wild, while the flowers of the forest are superior in beauty to any found in our native land. A few settlers from Sweden are already there, and some Hollanders. The native red men have hitherto proved friendly; and I trust by treating them kindly, with due regard to their just rights, we may ever remain on brotherly terms with them. They are mere wanderers over the land, build no cities, nor permanently cultivate the ground. I trust before to-morrow's sun has set, unless I am deceived, to obtain a grant of this territory, in lieu of a debt owing by the government to my father of nearly 15,000 pounds. I wish forthwith to despatch a vessel with certain commissioners authorised to purchase lands from the natives; and as Friend Mead has spoken favourably of thee, it is my wish to send thee with them. Wilt thou accept my offer? I will tell thee, if thou wilt, more particularly of thy duties."

Wenlock's heart somewhat sunk within him at this proposal. He had been hoping to make Mary Mead his wife; yet he was sure her father would not allow her to go forth into a new settlement, and to undergo all the incidental risks and hardships. How long a time might pass before he could return, he could not tell. Of one thing only he felt sure, that she would be faithful to him.

Some time had passed since he left Rotterdam, his friend Van Erk having given him permission to go over to England to enter the employment of William Mead. He had, since then, been living in his family, enjoying an almost daily intercourse with Mary; not yet, however, having obtained a position to enable him to marry her. Her father had resolved to put his patience and constancy to the test. Here, however, was a trial he had not expected; and when Penn had sent for him, he had, with the sanguine spirit of youth, hoped that it was to receive some appointment which would enable him to realise the wishes of his heart. Still the offer was a flattering one, and he felt that it would be unwise in him to decline it. He therefore, in suitable language, accepted the offer.

"Stay here then," said Penn, "as I have abundance of work for thee for some days to come, and I will then more fully explain to thee my wishes."

While Penn was still speaking, a messenger arrived from London. He brought a summons for him to attend a council at Whitehall, a note from a friend at court informing him that it was to settle the matter of the colony. He hastened up to London. In the council chamber were already assembled his majesty's privy councillors, and at the farther end of the room was the king himself, hat on head. William Penn, not the least conspicuous among them for his height and manly bearing, advanced up the room in his usual dignified manner; but neither did he doff his hat nor bend his knee before the king's majesty, although he has come in the hope of obtaining an object among the dearest to his heart.

"I have come at thy desire, and thank thee for the invitation," said Penn, standing before the king.

"Verily thou art welcome," said the monarch, with a smile on his lips; at the same time removing his hat and placing it by his side.

"Friend Charles, why dost thou not keep on thy hat?" said Penn with perfect gravity; at the same time making no attempt to remove his own.

"Ha! ha! ha! knowest thou not, Friend William, that it is the custom of this place for only one person to remain covered at a time?" answered the king, laughing heartily. "To business, however, my lords," he added. "And what name hast thou fixed on for this new province, Master Penn?"

"I have come at thy desire."

"As it is a somewhat mountainous country, I would have it called New Wales," answered the Quaker.

Here Master Secretary Blathwayte, who was a Welshman, interposed; in reality objecting to have the country of a sect to which he was no friend called after his native land.

"Well then, as it hath many noble forests, let it be called Sylvania," said Penn.

"Nay, nay; but I have a better name still," exclaimed the king. "We will call it Pennsylvania, in honour of your worthy father, — the great admiral. The forest land of Penn, that shall be it; and my word shall be as the law of the Medes and Persians."

At this the courtiers laughed, not, perchance, considering the king's word of much value. However, the name was thus fixed, the patent being then and there issued under the king's inspection.

With the charter in his possession, Penn returned home to make the final arrangements with Sidney for the great work he had undertaken. The document was written on a roll of parchment. At the head of the first sheet there is a well-executed portrait of Charles the Second, while the borders are handsomely emblazoned with heraldic devices. Great had been the opposition made to Penn's receiving this grant. Sidney had come back to Worminghurst.

"God hath given it to me in the face of the world," exclaimed Penn, as the friends met. "He will bless and make it the seed of a nation."

Truly has that prediction been fulfilled.

Chapter Thirteen.

Two fine vessels lay in mid stream a little way below London, with sails loosened, ready to take their departure. The wind was light, and they were waiting for the turn of the tide. Many boats surrounded them, and numerous visitors still thronged their decks. On board one of them was William Mead and his family.

Wenlock Christison held Mary's hand as her father was about to lead her to the side of the vessel, to descend into the boat.

"Thou wilt be supported, Wenlock, if thou dost look whence support can alone be gained," said Mary; "and my father has promised that when thou dost return he will no longer withhold me from thee. What more can I say? Thou dost know my love, and I have faith in thee."

"Thanks, Mary, for those words," said Wenlock. "I trust I may do my duty, and soon return to thee."

Thus the young Quaker and his betrothed parted. The other visitors quitted the good ship *Amity*, and her consort the *John Sarah*, which now, with sails sheeted home, slowly glided down the Thames. They made but slight progress, however, as they had frequently to come to an anchor before they altogether got clear of the river. They then proceeded once more without interruption until they reached Plymouth Sound. Here they took in more provisions. On board the *Amity* also there came a passenger, who announced himself as Master Jonas Ford, the son of the factor of the Irish estates of Mr William Penn. He brought a letter. He was a Quaker, his figure slight, his cheeks smooth. His dress, his language, and manners were equally correct. Yet Wenlock did not feel attracted towards him. Jonas Ford, however, seemed determined to obtain his friendship, and from the first attached himself especially to him.

"Hast ever crossed the ocean before, young sir?" said honest Richard Dinan, captain of the *Amity*, addressing Wenlock. "You seem to have a pair of sea legs of your own."

"Yea, verily, friend. I served on board a man-of-war, and saw no little service," answered Wenlock.

"Then how didst thou quit it? It is an honest calling, to my mind," observed the captain.

"Why, by being blown up and left floating alone on the water. Verily I thought that was a sufficient sign to me no longer to engage in carnal warfare."

"Oh, ay, I see. You have joined friend Penn. Well, well, each man to his taste. However, I guessed you had served at sea directly I saw you walking the deck."

After this, Captain Dinan paid considerable attention to Wenlock,— much more so, indeed, than he did to Jonas Ford. Altogether there were about twenty passengers on board the *Amity*, with a crew of forty men. She also carried guns, to be able to defend herself against Algerine rovers, or West Indian pirates, of whom there were not a few roving those seas at that time. Prince Rupert and his brother had made piracy somewhat fashionable during the days of the Commonwealth, and there were not wanting a few lawless spirits to follow their example.

For some time the voyage continued prosperous, though, as the wind was light, the progress of the two emigrant ships was but slow. One day Wenlock had gone forward, when a seaman, whose furrowed countenance, thickly covered with scars and grey locks, showing the hard service he had gone through during a long life, addressed him.

"I know your name, Master Christison," he said, "for I served under a man who I think was your father. It was many years ago; but yet I remember his looks and tone of voice, as you remind me of him. He saved my life, and did more than save my life, for he prevented me from becoming a hardened ruffian like many of my companions." On this the old seaman ran on, and gave him many accounts of his father, to which Wenlock listened with deep interest. "Well, sir," said the old man, "whenever you have time to listen to a yarn, if I happen to be below, just send for old Bill Rullock." Wenlock promised the old man that he would not fail to come and talk to him, hoping indeed, as in duty bound, to put the truth before him.

The two ships were now about ten days' sail from the American continent. Wenlock was walking the deck with Captain Dinan, most of the other passengers having gone to their cabins, for the sea was somewhat high, and the wind had increased. Dark clouds also were rising in the north-west, and driving rapidly across the sky.

"I do not altogether like the look of the weather," observed the captain. "I see Captain Smith is shortening sail; we must do the same:" and he forthwith summoned the crew to perform that operation.

Scarcely were the men off the yards, when the wind, as if suddenly let loose, struck the ship with terrific fury, throwing her on her beam ends. Many of the passengers cried out for fear, thinking that she was going down. Among those who exhibited the greatest terror was Jonas Ford, who wrung his hands, bitterly repenting that he had ever come to sea. The captain issued his orders in a clear voice, which the crew readily obeyed, Wenlock giving his assistance.

"Cut away the mizen mast," cried the captain.

A glittering axe soon descended on the stout mast, while the active crew cleared the shrouds and all the other ropes, the mast falling clear of the ship into the foaming ocean. Still she lay helpless in the trough of the sea.

"The mainmast must go," cried the captain.

"The mainmast must go."

That too was cut away. The ship instantly felt the relief, and now rising to an even keel, she flew before the furious gale. Those on board had been so taken up with their own dangerous condition, that no one thought of looking out for their consort.

When, however, the most imminent danger was over, Wenlock cast his eye in the direction in which she had last been seen. In vain he looked out on either side; no sail was visible. Others also now began to make inquiries for the *John Sarah*. Many had friends on board. Too probably, struck by the furious blast, she had gone down. Sad were the forebodings of all as to her fate. Such might have been theirs. Human nature is sadly selfish, and many were rather inclined to congratulate themselves on their escape, than to mourn for the supposed fate of their countrymen.

On, on flew the *Amity* towards the south, far away from the Delaware, from the land to which she was bound. The dark foam-crested seas rose up on every side, hissing and roaring, and threatening to overwhelm her. Still the brave captain kept up his courage, and endeavoured to keep up that of those on board.

"We must get jury-masts up," he said, "when the storm abates; and plying to the north, endeavour to regain the ground we have lost."

"Verily we had a fierce gale, friend Christison," said Ford, coming up to Wenlock when the weather once more moderated. "Didst not thou fear greatly?"

"No," answered Wenlock; "though it seemed to me that the ship might probably go down."

"Ah! truly, I felt very brave too," said Ford.

"You took an odd way of showing it," answered Wenlock, who had observed the abject fear into which his companion had been thrown.

"Ah! yea, I might have somewhat trembled, but that was more for the thought of others than for myself," said Ford. "And now tell me, when dost thou think we shall arrive at our destination?"

"That is more than any one on board can say," said Wenlock; "but we must do all that men can do, and leave the rest to Him who rules the sea!"

All hands were now engaged in getting the ship to rights. Scarcely however had jury-masts been set up, than signs of another storm appeared in the sky.

"I like not the look of the weather," observed the captain. "Christison, your eyes are sharp; is that a sail away to the north-east?"

"Yes, verily," answered Wenlock.

"Can it be our consort?"

"No; she would not appear in that quarter. She is a stranger, and seems to be coming rapidly on towards us," observed Wenlock, after watching her for little time. "A tall ship too, I suspect."

Captain Dinan had hoped before this to haul up to the wind, but the increasing gale made this impossible. As, however, he was going out of his course, he only carried as much sail as necessity required. The stranger therefore came quickly up with the *Amity*. The captain now began to eye her very narrowly.

"I like not her looks," he observed. "She is a war ship, and yet shows no colours."

The captain asked his officers their opinion. They agreed with him. Bill Rullock, who was a man of experience, was called aft.

"I have little doubt about it," he observed. "That craft's a pirate, and we must keep clear of her if we would escape having to walk the plank or getting our throats cut." Nearer and nearer drew the stranger.

"Rather than surrender we must fight to the last," observed the sturdy captain. "Christison, Ford, which will you all do, gentlemen?" he asked, addressing the passengers.

"Verily, I will go below and hide myself," said Ford. "It becometh not one of my creed to engage in mortal combat."

"If you order me to work a gun, I will do so," answered Wenlock. "Albeit peace is excellent and blessed, and warfare is accursed, yet I cannot see that it would be my duty to allow others to fight for the defence of my life which I will not defend myself; or, for lack of fighting, to allow myself or those who look to men to protect them, — the women and children on board, — to be destroyed by outlawed ruffians such as are probably those on board yonder ship."

Chapter Fourteen.

As soon as the captain of the *Amity* was convinced of the character of the stranger, he set all the sail the ship would carry, yet hoping to escape from her. Looking to windward however, he saw that they had an enemy to contend with, as much to be dreaded, in their crippled condition, as the pirate ship. His experienced eye told him that another hurricane was about to break. Part of the crew, and most of the passengers also, were standing at the guns, the remainder of the crew being required to work the sails. The courage showed by all on board gave the captain hopes of being able to beat off the enemy. On came the tall ship. As Wenlock watched her, he could not help perceiving that she was of overpowering force.

"Stand by to shorten sail," cried the captain. His eye had been fixed on a dark cloud, which came flying like some messenger of destruction across the sky.

"You must be smart, lads," cried old Bill Rullock, "if you have no fancy for being sent to Davy Jones's locker before you are many minutes older." The old man set an example by his activity.

Nearer and nearer drew the pirate, for such, there was no doubt, was the character of the stranger. A bright flash issued from her bows, and a shot came bounding over the water towards the *Amity*. On this Captain Dinan ordered the English flag to be hoisted. Scarcely had it flown out when another shot followed. Still, neither hit the ship. As the first flash was seen, Jonas Ford was observed to dive below.

"Our friend is as good as his word," observed the captain, laughing. "If any others wish to follow his example, let them go at once, for we may have warm work ere long. To my mind, though I am a plain man, a person should so live as not to fear the lightning's flash, nor the foeman's shot, nor the raging ocean either; and then, whether in tempest or battle, he will be able to do his duty like a man, knowing that there is One above who will look after him, and, if He thinks fit, carry him through all dangers."

Shot after shot followed. Now one went through the ship's sails; now one passed on one side, now on the other; but none did any material harm. Still, Captain Dinan gave no order to fire in return. Thus for some time the ships continued to sail on, the pirate gradually drawing nearer. At length she yawed and let fly her whole broadside. Several shots struck the *Amity*, two poor fellows being killed, and a third wounded. The faces of many of the passengers, on this grew pale, yet they stood firmly at their quarters. And now, once more, the pirate kept on her coarse. Still Captain Dinan would not fire.

"Christison," said the captain, "we have someone who knows better how to fight for us than we do ourselves. See! if the pirate attempts that manoeuvre again, he will pay dearly for it."

So eagerly, it seemed, were the pirates watching their expected prize, that they had not observed the rapid approach of the dark cloud. Once more the pirate yawed. At that instant a loud roar was heard, and the hurricane broke over the two ships. The flashes of the guns were seen, but none of the shots struck the *Amity*; all were buried in the ocean. Over went the tall ship, her masts level with the ocean. The crew of the *Amity*, at a signal from their captain, had lowered most of their sails; and now away she flew, leaving the pirate ship apparently on the point of sinking beneath the waves. They were seen leaping and roaring round her; but even had those on board the *Amity* desired to render their fellow-creatures assistance, they would have had no power to do so. The hurricane increased in fury, and often it seemed as if the *Amity* herself would go down. Tossed and buffeted by the seas, the water poured in through many a leak. The pumps were manned, and all the passengers were summoned to work them. Some, however, complained of sickness, and retired to their berths. Among them was Jonas Ford.

"Nay, though our friend finds it against his conscience to fight, he shall, at all events, labour at the pumps," exclaimed the captain, ordering three of the seamen to fetch him up. "Will you go also, Master Christison? Perchance you can persuade him more easily; but I can take no refusal."

After searching for some time, Ford was found concealed in the hold, into which he had crawled. The water, however, coming in, had somewhat frightened him, and he was just creeping out of his concealment. Not unwillingly, Wenlock brought him on deck, and assigned him a place at one of the pumps. There he was compelled to labour. Once he attempted to escape below, but Bill Rullock caught sight of him, and quickly brought him back; and he was kept labouring, uttering moans and groans at his hard fate. All night long the ship ran on. Another day and another night followed, and yet the wind blew furiously as ever, and with difficulty could she be kept afloat. While the gale continued there was no hope of getting at the leaks. Many of the seamen and some of the officers began to look grave.

"Depend upon it our time has come," said the second mate to Wenlock. "I have had enough of the world, and have been knocked about in it so roughly, that I care but little."

"Our times, we are told, are in God's hands," answered Wenlock, calmly.

Wenlock, who had been taking his spell at the pumps, walked aft.

"We are in the latitude of the West India Islands," observed the captain. "Any hour we may make land, and a bright look-out must be kept for it."

Experienced seamen were aloft straining their eyes ahead and on either bow. At length a voice came from the foretopmast-head, "Land! land!"

"Where away?" cried the captain.

"On the starboard bow," was the answer.

"What does it look like?"

"A low land with tall trees," replied the seaman from aloft.

Two of the mates went up to look at it. They gave the same description. The captain examined his chart.

"Bill Rullock says he has been there," observed the first mate.

Bill Rullock was sent for.

"Do you know anything of the land ahead?" asked the captain.

"I think I do, sir," was the answer; "and that craft which chased us the other day knew it too, I have an idea. To my mind, she also would have been looking in there before long; but if she has gone to the bottom there is no fear of that, and we shall find shelter and wood and water and plenty of turtle, and the means of repairing our ship."

"Is there a harbour there, then?" asked the captain.

"As good a one as you can desire, sir," said Bill; "and if it please you, I can take the ship in."

As the crew were nearly worn out with pumping, and the water, notwithstanding, still gained on the ship, the captain determined to take the *Amity* into the harbour of which Bill Rullock spoke. The ship was therefore kept away for the island, Bill Rullock taking charge of her as pilot. He at once showed by his calm manner and the steady course he steered that he knew well what he was about. As the ship drew nearer the island, it appeared to be larger and higher than was at first supposed, and covered with cocoa-nut and other trees. Rounding a point, a narrow opening appeared. The ship's head was directed toward it, and, guided by the old seaman, she passed safely through it, though it seemed as if an active man could have leaped on shore from either side. So clear, too, was the water, that the bottom could be seen below the ship's keel. The order to "furl sails" was given, and the ship came to an anchor in a broad lagoon, where she could lie secure from the fiercest hurricanes of those regions. On one side was a sandy beach, where the old sailor assured the captain the ship could be placed on shore with safety, when her damages might be examined. The trees came close down to the water's edge, and among them were seen several huts, and ruins of huts, showing that the spot had at one time been inhabited, but no persons appeared. Hauled up on shore, too, were several boats, one or two in good repair, but the others considerably damaged. Broken anchors, spars, pieces of cable, and other ship's gear lay scattered about, confirming the account given by old Rullock. As there was no time to be lost, the passengers immediately went on shore, and they and the crew set to work to land their goods as well as the cargo, that the ship, being lightened, might be hauled up for repair. The ruined huts were repaired, and others were built, so as to afford shelter to the passengers while this operation was going on. Every one worked with a will, with the exception of two or three, Jonas Ford being one of them. He grumbled greatly at having the voyage thus prolonged, and not ceasing to blame the captain for the ship having failed to reach the Delaware at the time expected. From a slight elevation near the harbour, a view of the whole sea on that side of the island could be obtained. Old Rullock had not been quite easy since their arrival. He had found evident traces of a late visit of persons to the island, and he confided to Wenlock his fears that should the vessel which had chased them have escaped, she might possibly come into that harbour to repair damages.

One morning, soon after daybreak, and before the men were called to their work, Rullock came hurrying into the village. Wenlock was the first person he met.

"It is as I feared," he said. "I have just made out a tall ship standing towards the island. Come and see her, and then let us ask the captain to decide what he will do. I advise that we should bring the guns down to the mouth of the harbour and defend it to the last. If those are the people I fear, they will give us no quarter; and if we yield, it will be only to have our throats cut, or to be thrown to the sharks."

On reaching the look-out place, Wenlock saw the ship of which the old seaman spoke. She was yet a long way off, and, as far as he could judge, was very like the vessel that had chased them.

The whole party were quickly astir. The captain determined to follow the old sailor's advice, and even the Quakers among the passengers agreed that they had no resource but to defend themselves, should the stranger prove to be the pirate they dreaded. As she approached the island, she must have discovered the English flag flying from the *Amity's* masthead; for instantly her own dark symbol was run up, and a shot was fired from her side, as if in defiance.

Happily, the wind, which had been light, prevented her from entering the harbour. As she passed by, however, the number of guns seen from her sides showed that she would be a formidable antagonist, and that she could scarcely be prevented, with a favourable breeze, from entering the harbour. The whole of the morning the party were kept in anxious expectation of what would occur, the pirate being seen to tack every now and then to keep her position off the land. At length a breeze from the sea set in, and once more she was seen approaching the harbour. Nearer and nearer she drew. All eyes were kept turned towards the dreaded object. In a brief time they might all be engaged in a deadly struggle, while the fate of the poor women and children was dreadful to contemplate. The captain and several of his officers were collected on the mound, watching the progress of the pirate.

"See, sir! see!" exclaimed Wenlock. "What say you to that?" and he pointed towards the sails of a lofty ship which at that instant appeared rounding a distant point of the island.

Chapter Fifteen.

The pirate had descried the stranger; for now her yards were seen to be braced up, and instead of standing towards the island, she tacked and stood again out to sea, her pirate flag still flying from her peak. As the stranger drew nearer, she was seen to be a much larger ship. Wenlock at once declared her to be a man-of-war; and this was soon seen to be the case, by the pennants and ensigns she hoisted. And now she was observed to be making more sail, and standing towards the pirate, which was evidently endeavouring to escape. The latter, however, in a short time, either considering escape impossible, or confiding in her own strength, again tacked, and stood boldly towards the man-of-war. Nearer and nearer they drew to each other. It was evident, from the pirate keeping her flag flying, that she intended to fight to the last. She was the first to fire, discharging her whole broadside at the man-of-war. The latter fired not a shot in return, but stood on, gradually shortening sail. Then suddenly luffing up, she crossed the bows of the pirate. As she did so, before the other could keep away, she fired her whole broadside, raking the pirate's decks fore and aft. The latter, again keeping away, fired in return, but little damage seemed to be done. The crew of the *Amity* set up a loud shout as they saw the success of their friends. And now the combatants, shrouded in smoke, stood away from the land, the rapid sound of their guns showing the desperation with which they were fighting. Those on shore watched them anxiously. Many a prayer was offered up for the success of the royal cruiser. Their own safety, indeed, depended on it. Farther and farther the combatants receded from the shore, till it was difficult to distinguish one from the other. Now they were shrouded with smoke, now the wind blew it away, and they were seen, still standing on, exchanging shots. Now at length they appeared locked in a close embrace. Then a dense mass of smoke was seen to ascend from their midst, followed by flames, and the loud sound of an explosion; but which was the sufferer it was impossible to discover, or whether both were involved in the same ruin. How earnestly, how anxiously they were watched from the shore! Now, at length, once more they were seen returning towards the island; but one was leading, the other apparently being towed astern. Which was the conqueror? was the question. On they came, nearer and nearer. Some declared that the pirate was the leading ship, and seemed ready to *give* way to despair.

"No, friends, no," exclaimed the captain. "I can assure you that yonder tall ship, although her spars and rigging are somewhat shattered by the fight, is the royal cruiser."

That he was right was soon made evident. Captain Dinan now ordered the boats to be got ready, and he, with Bill Rullock, accompanied by Wenlock and one of his mates, went out in order to assist in piloting in the king's ship. The latter shortened sail to allow the boat to come alongside. The deck showed the fierce combat in which she had been engaged. The bulwarks were shattered; the decks ploughed up, and stained with blood; and numbers of the crew were going about with their heads and limbs bound up with handkerchiefs, while several bodies lay stretched out on the deck, a flag hastily thrown over them, partly concealing their forms. On one side stood a wretched group, their arms lashed behind them with ropes, and stripped to the waist, covered with smoke and blood. They were some of the survivors, it was evident, of the pirate crew. Captain Dinan, accompanied by Wenlock went aft to speak to the captain. The countenance of the latter, a fine, dignified-looking man, Wenlock at once recognised. He advanced towards him. He started when he saw Wenlock.

"Why, my friend!" he exclaimed, "I little expected ever to see you again!"

"Nor I you, Sir Richard. I thought you had perished on the fatal day when the *Royal James* blew up."

"No; thanks to you, my life was spared; for after we were parted, I was picked up by an English boat."

Sir Richard Haddock informed Wenlock that he had come out as commodore to the American station. His ship was the *Leopard*, of fifty-four guns.

"The pirates fought well," he observed; "and as many perished in attempting to blow up the ship, we shall have but few to hand over to the executioner when we arrive in Virginia, whither I am now bound."

As both ships, after the action, required a good deal of repair, the commodore accepted Captain Dinan's offer of piloting him into the harbour. It was a trial to Wenlock to find himself once more among his former associates; for he had met several of the officers of the *Leopard* when serving under Lord Ossory. They, however, treated his opinions with respect. In truth, thanks to the courage and talents exhibited by William Penn, the character of the sect had been raised considerably in the opinion of the public of late; albeit, there were many who were ready to ridicule and persecute them on occasion. Happily, too, there was no time for idleness, as officers and crew were engaged from sunrise to sunset in repairing the damaged ships.

One day, old Rullock came up to Wenlock, who had gone alone a little distance from the village.

"I do not know what you think of that young gentleman, Master Ford," said Rullock; "but I have an idea that he is a rogue in grain, and a fool into the bargain, as many rogues are. He was so frightened in the hurricane that he does not want to go to sea again. I heard him talking the other day with three or four passengers and several of the crew about a plan he had proposed to remain behind. They have a notion that if they were to set the *Amity* on fire before we get the cargo on board, the captain would only be too glad to leave those who might wish to stay behind; he going off in the *Leopard*, or the pirate ship. Master Ford thinks, as the chief part of the stores would be left behind, they would have the advantage of them. They have induced three or four silly young women to promise to remain with them. Of course, the plan of burning the ship is a secret. Soon after I heard the precious plan, they invited me to join them;

because, knowing that I had been an evil-doer, they thought I should have no scruple about the matter."

Wenlock, on hearing this, immediately sought the captain.

"It would be very easy to prevent these plans being carried out," he said; "but what to do with Ford and his companions is more difficult."

The captain took the matter very coolly.

"We will just pick out Master Ford and three or four of the ringleaders, and clap them into limbo, and depend upon it they will not further attempt to carry out their plan," he observed.

This was done forthwith by a party of soldiers from the ship of war, for whom Wenlock had applied to Sir Richard Haddock. No further time was now lost in getting the cargo on board. Ford and his companions had been kept in durance vile in a hut by themselves, and a guard placed over them. Sir Richard and Captain Dinan, and some other officers, visited them together.

"Now, my friends," said the captain, "you have your choice. If you desire to remain here, you are welcome to do so, but neither stores nor provisions can we afford you. Otherwise, you will return on board the ship, and, when we arrive in Pennsylvania, the matter will be submitted to the proper authorities."

As Ford's companions were three of the greatest ruffians among the crew, he, dreading to be left with them, entreated that he might be allowed to return on board. They, however, wished to remain.

"No, no!" said the captain. "We did not give you your choice. You are good seamen, and are wanted to work the ship. You were misled by this silly young man, and therefore will return on board with us."

The three ships were at length in a condition for sea. The pirates' ship was sent out first, navigated by some of the officers and crew of the *Leopard*. The *Amity* followed, the king's ship coming last, and the wind being favourable, all three steered a course for Virginia; the *Amity* afterwards to continue her voyage to the Delaware.

Chapter Sixteen.

The good ship *Amity* was sailing up the magnificent stream of the Delaware. Her progress, however, was not without impediment, as huge masses of ice came floating down, lately broken up by the warm sun of the early spring.

"There's your future home, my friends," said the captain, pointing to the left side of the coast; "but it will take us some time before we can reach the spot where our friends have settled. On the right we have West New Jersey, where, owing to Master William Penn, a new free colony was settled some time ago; but that is but a small portion of the territory compared with Pennsylvania. I went out as mate in the *Kent*, commanded by Captain Gregory Marlow. We carried out the first settlers and the commissioners. They were nearly all Quakers, and a very good sort of people they were. I remember, just as we sailed from the Thames, the king coming alongside, and nothing would satisfy him but that he must come on board; whereupon he gave us his blessing. Whether it was of much value or not, it is not for me to say; but whether or not, we reached port in safety. Several other ships followed. The commissioners bought land of the natives, and established friendly relations with them; and if you were to go on shore there now, you would find as prosperous a community as any in the world." The new settlers, on hearing this account, looked with greater interest on the far distant shores of the land to which the captain pointed. On either side tall forests rose up, —a thick barrier to the country beyond.

"Ay, friends," continued the captain, "it is a fine land, but you will have many a tall tree to cut down before you can grow wheat and barley out of it; and for those who love work, there is work enough before them, not only for them, but for their children, and children's children after them, and no fear of the country being too thickly peopled."

At length, on a point of land an opening in the forest was seen, with numerous log huts and other buildings of more pretensions below the tall trees. It was the town of Newcastle, lately established. However, as the wind was favourable, and the captain was anxious to reach his destination, he declined staying there, but sailed on farther up the river. Each reach of the stream presented some fresh views, greatly by their beauty delighting the new comers. At length, two vessels were seen moored off a town on the west bank, which the captain informed them was the Swedish settlement of Upland. All eyes were directed towards them. As they approached, the captain declared his belief that one of them was the *John Sarah*, and in a short time the *Amity* came to anchor close to her. She had fortunately, when the hurricane came on, by furling her sails in time, escaped injury, and had thus been able to haul up, and gain the mouth of the Delaware. On proceeding up the stream, however, she and the *Bristol Factor*, the other ship, had been frozen up where they now were. There was a pleasant meeting of friends, and all going on shore, offered up their thanks to Heaven together, for their safe arrival and preservation from so many dangers. The village off which the *Amity* had brought up had been built by a number of Friends, who had arrived in the country several years before. The site they had chosen was a good one, and many believed that it would be the future capital of the colony. The scene was very wild, albeit highly picturesque. Many of the inhabitants of the new settlement, unable to build houses, had dug caves in the banks of the river, in which they had taken up their abodes, roofing over the front part with pieces of timber and boughs. From early dawn till sunset the woodman's axe was at work felling the tall trees. At night these were piled up, with the branches and lighter wood beneath; huge fires being kindled as the most rapid way of disposing of them. Primitive ploughs were at work between the stumps of the trees, turning up the ground for receiving grain, both of wheat and Indian corn, while the spade was also wielded by those preparing gardens. Many languages were heard spoken, while the costumes of the settlers were still more varied. The dusky forms of the Indians also were to be seen collected round the settlers, with their painted faces, their feathered head-dresses, and costumes of skin ornamented with thread of various colours. Numerous sawpits had been formed, and sawyers were at work preparing planks for the buildings. Already many houses had been run up, with high gables, gaily ornamented with paint and rough carving; for the Swedish settlers had been there already nearly forty years. The somewhat romantic notions entertained by Wenlock and his younger fellow passengers were rather rudely dissipated on their arrival. The work of settling he soon found was a plain matter-of-fact business, requiring constant and persevering labour. Some of the settlers remained at the town, others proceeded farther up the river to a spot near the confluence of the two rivers Schuylkill and Delaware. Wenlock, however, resolved to wait the arrival of Colonel Markham, who had gone out as chief agent and commissioner for his cousin, the governor, some months before. He was now, with his staff, some distance off, surveying the province. Although not a Quaker, he was greatly trusted by William Penn, as a man of dauntless courage, talent, and perseverance. Soon after landing, old Bill Rullock came up to Wenlock. "I have a favour to ask," he said. "I have knocked about at sea all my life till I am weary of it. I heard your addresses and those of others on board, and I have made up my mind to turn Quaker. I want you, therefore, to get my discharge from the captain. I could run from the ship, of course, but that would not be a good way of beginning my new career; so if I cannot leave with a proper discharge, I must go to sea again. If it is God's will that my old carcase should become food for fishes, I must submit to it; but I have truly a great fancy for ending my days in these green woods." Wenlock promised to make interest with Captain Dinan.

"I shall be sorry to lose him," answered the captain; "but he deserves a reward for the service he rendered us, and it would be hard to take him off again to sea against his will. Here is his discharge, and his pay up to the present time."

The old seaman was highly delighted when Wenlock told him that he was free.

"And, now, another favour I have to ask is, that I may stick fast by you. I have still got plenty of work in me, and I should like to serve you as long as I live. There is another person, however, I should not like to serve, and that is Jonas Ford."

Ford had behaved so cunningly during the voyage from the West Indies, that he had considerably lessened the suspicions against him. He had assured Captain Dinan that he had no thoughts of committing the crime of which he had been accused; that the words he had uttered, overheard by Rullock, had reference to an entirely different matter. As Rullock, indeed, was the only witness against him, and as even the other accused persons did not criminate him, the captain came to the determination of proceeding no further in the business. He was, therefore, set at liberty, and landed with the other passengers. His companions were also liberated, as they had committed no overt act, and there was no evidence against them. Ford, who had all along protested his innocence, tried to worm his way into the confidence of Wenlock, and always volunteered to accompany him whenever he made any excursions into the interior. Wenlock, in spite of the young man's professions, disliked him more and more. Still he could not altogether get rid of him. With the aid of old Rullock, Wenlock had built a hut for himself in the neighbourhood of Upland, and he purposed awaiting there the arrival of Colonel Markham. Hearing, however, at length, that the colonel was within the distance of five days' march, though he had had but little experience in traversing the American forests, he yet — by noting the appearance of the bark on the trees, by the aid of the sun during the day, and by certain marks which the surveyors had made—believed that he should have no great difficulty in reaching the colonel's camp. Rullock, of course, wished to attend him.

"No, my friend," he answered; "you stay at home and take care of the house. I am strong, and well accustomed to exercise; but, depend upon it, you would knock up with the fatigue."

The old man was at length obliged to acknowledge that Wenlock was right, and to submit. Two or three of the old settlers advised him to take a guide, pointing out the difficulties of traversing the forest; but he, confident in his own knowledge, persisted in his determination. Staff in hand, with knapsack on his back, he set forth. It did occur to him, perhaps, that he should be more at his ease had he possessed a brace of pistols or a musket; but his profession prohibited their use as a means of defence, and he declined accepting some arms from a friendly Swede, who offered them. The weather was fine, and he had learned the art of camping out. Starting early, he marched on bravely all day, believing himself to be in the right course. Once or twice he stopped to rest, and then again proceeded on. At night, collecting a supply of birch-bark, as he had seen the Indians do, he built himself a wigwam. Abundance of fuel was at hand, and, lighting his fire, he cooked some provisions he had brought with him. After this, commending himself to the care of Heaven, he lay down in his wigwam, and was soon fast asleep. The following day he journeyed on in like manner. Clouds, however, obscured the sky, and more than once he doubted whether he was continuing in the right direction. The third day came, and he pushed onwards, but before he encamped at night, he felt sure that he must have diverged greatly from the right path. Still believing that he might recover it the following day, he lay down to rest. His provisions, however, ran somewhat short; indeed, he had miscalculated the amount he should require. At length the fifth day came: his food was expended, and he had to confess that he had entirely lost his path. The whole day he wandered on, endeavouring to regain it. At last he got into what appeared an Indian path. He followed it up, but in the end found that it only led to a spot where an encampment had once stood—now deserted. He had been suffering greatly from thirst, even more than from hunger. To stay still might seal his fate. Onward, therefore, he pushed. At length, however, from want of food and water, his strength failed him. His sight grew dim, and, fainting, he fell on the ground. How long he had lain there he knew not, when he heard a strange, deep-toned, sonorous voice. Languidly he opened his eyes, and saw standing over him a tall Indian, of dignified appearance and full costume of paint and feathers.

"Who are you?" asked Wenlock, dreamily.

"I am Taminent, chief sachem of the red men of this country," answered the Indian, who, stooping down as he spoke, raised him in his arms.

"He saw standing over him a tall Indian."

Chapter Seventeen.

The Indian chief, applying a leathern bottle to Wenlock's mouth, poured some water down his throat. It greatly revived him.

"I see white skin want food," said the chief. Saying this, he produced a cake of Indian corn, which Wenlock eagerly devoured.

"Now, come; I will take you with me," said Taminent, in more perfect English than Wenlock had expected to hear; and, supporting him in his arms, the chief led him along a path into which they quickly entered. After going some distance, an open space amid the trees appeared, and within it a collection of tall birch-bark wigwams of a conical shape. A number of women were seated in front of the huts, while children were playing about. On one side, the ground had been turned up, evidently for the reception of Indian corn or other seed, while stretched between poles were the skins of animals, the bodies of others being hung up over fires to dry in the smoke. As soon as the chief was seen, the women rose from their seats, and a number of men came out of the tents to welcome him. He introduced Wenlock in a few words, which the latter did not understand.

"Come," said the chief, "wigwam ready. You rest;" and leading him to an unoccupied hut, he pointed to the interior, the floor of which was covered with a number of handsomely-woven mats. On one side was a pile of small twigs and leaves. This was spread out, and a mat placed on the top of it. The chief then made signs to Wenlock that he should rest there. He seemed well-pleased when Wenlock threw himself down on the couch.

"There; you rest," he said. "No harm come to white skin;" and, covering him with a mat, he retired, drawing a curtain across the entrance of the wigwam. Wenlock slept soundly for some hours, feeling perfectly secure under the protection of the chief. On awaking, he found that it was already dark, but the sounds of voices outside the wigwam showed him that the Indians had not yet retired to rest. On drawing aside the curtain, he saw several fires lighted, over which women were presiding with pots and spits, on which birds and small animals were being cooked. Close to the entrance a warrior was seated on a mat, as if keeping guard. No sooner did he observe Wenlock, than he rose up and ran off, apparently to inform the chief that his guest was awake. Taminent soon after appeared, and invited Wenlock to take his seat on the ground. Immediately several women came up with various dishes of roast and boiled food, with cakes of maize. Pure water, poured from a skin bottle, was their only beverage. Happily the fire-water had not yet been introduced among the red men, — that fearful poison which has destroyed thousands and tens of thousands of their race. While the chief and his guest were seated at their repast, an Indian came up to them, and addressed the former, who, in return, apparently gave some directions. Wenlock observed the Indians employed in making a couple of rough litters, with which a party of them started away. In a short time they returned, bearing between them a couple of persons, who were brought up and placed near the fire. Wenlock at once recognised the features of Ford, while in the other man he discovered one of the seamen of the *Amity*, who had been connected with Ford's plot to burn the ship. They were both in an exhausted state; indeed, it seemed to Wenlock that Ford especially could scarcely recover. He at once suspected that they had been by some means lost in the forest, and were suffering from exhaustion, as he had been. The Indian chief, taking upon himself the office of doctor, poured some water down their throats, and then gave them a small quantity of food. Both somewhat revived. The seaman, indeed, in a short time was able to sit up. To Wenlock's questions, however, as to how he had come into that condition, he would make no reply, except saying, while he pointed to his companion —

"He took me; he will tell you all about it. I came as his servant, and a pretty mess he led me into."

Wenlock then begged that Ford might be placed on the couch he had occupied, feeling sure that perfect rest was what he most of all now required. He explained to the chief, also, that a little food at a time was more likely to restore him than a large quantity taken at once. The two men were accordingly carried into the wigwam, while some of the Indians brought in a further supply of leaves and mats, to make a bed for Wenlock. The chief then signified to him that three squaws would sit up and prepare food, that he might give it to his countrymen as he thought fit. Night was drawing on, when the loud barking of dogs announced that some stranger was approaching the camp.

"Hallo! I am glad I have found some living men at last," exclaimed a voice which Wenlock thought sounded very like that of old Rullock.

"I pray thee, friends, call in your beasts, or maybe they will be taking a mouthful out of my legs, seeing that there is but little covering to them—thanks to the bushes. Hallo! I say, friends, red men!"

The Indians, who had lain down in their wigwams, now got up, and hurried forth to meet the newcomer, followed by Wenlock, who had no longer any doubt as to who he was. A torch, lighted at one of the fires, which were not yet extinguished, was carried by one of the Indians, who at the same time, called in the dogs. Its light fell on Wenlock's countenance. The old man started.

"Hurrah!" he exclaimed. "Verily, I am truly glad to see thee alive and well, friend Christison. I have a long yarn to spin into thine ear, but it is as well that our red friends shall not hear it. They might not hold the white skins in quite as much respect as they now do."

"Thou art right, friend Rullock. Hold thy peace about it now," said Wenlock. "I am glad to see thee, and thou wilt receive a hearty welcome from our red brothers in this encampment. There are two white men also here;" and Wenlock told him the way in which Jonas Ford and his companion had been brought into the camp.

"Ah, verily! the scoundrels would only have got their deserts if they had been left in the woods," answered the old sailor, who did his best to speak in Quaker fashion, but did not always succeed. "Hark thee, friend Christison. Those two villains had formed a plot to follow thee; and if they had found thee alone and unprepared, to have put thee to death."

"Impossible!" answered Wenlock. "Ford is a weak, cowardly young man; but I do not think that he would be willingly guilty of such a crime."

"I tell thee, I overheard them plotting to murder thee!" persisted the old man. "I had thoughts of getting some one as my companion to go after them, but as you had gone, and they were just setting out, I thought I might be too late; so taking my well-tried musket, and trusting that my old legs would carry me as well as their young ones,

I set out in their track, hoping to come up with them before they could overtake you."

"I thank thee heartily, friend Rullock; but they are fellow-creatures, and I will try to soften Ford's heart by heaping 'coals of fire upon his head.' They will see you, and guess what your coming means; but we will say nothing about it, and only for prudence sake keep an eye on their proceedings. When you see them both almost on the point of death, you will feel inclined to have compassion on them."

"I shall be inclined to think that a certain person, who is nameless, has been baulked of his prey," answered the old sailor. "However, it's not for me to lay hands on them, villains though they are; but I hope that thou wilt bring them up before. Colonel Markham, or Master Penn when he comes out."

"That would not be the best way of heaping coals of fire on their heads," answered Wenlock. "No, no; if they had evil intentions against me, they have been frustrated; and God will look after me in future, as He has done heretofore."

The chief, who was among those risen, received the old sailor with great kindness, and ordering some food to be prepared for him, told him that he was to consider himself a brother, and rest assured that he would be treated as such as long as he chose to remain with them.

Rullock, having gone through a good deal of fatigue, soon fell asleep after his supper, and left Wenlock the chief charge of attending to the other two white men. By the morning, Ford was considerably better. His companion, who was still stronger, wished to persuade him to return to the settlement, but it was very evident that he would be unable to perform such a journey.

"Be at rest, friends," said Wenlock to them. "Whatever might have been the cause of thy coming out into the forest, be not anxious about it. I will treat thee as if thou wert my dearest brother. More, surely, thou canst not desire."

"O Christison, I am very different from thee," answered Ford, for a moment some better feeling rising in his bosom. Cowardice, however, and want of confidence in others, made him very quickly add: "I harbour no ill-will against any man. I had been anxious to see something of the country, and finding that thou hadst started, I wished to join thee. Thou canst not suppose that I should ever harbour any other feeling than affection and regard for thee."

The day was drawing on, and most of the Indians had gone forth to hunt, or to tend some cultivated ground in another part of the forest, when a messenger arrived, bringing the information to Taminent, that the white chief was coming to his camp. On hearing this, Taminent and the principal men retired to their wigwams, and in a short time came forth dressed in full Indian costume, with feathers in their hair, their cheeks painted, and their dress ornamented with a variety of devices.

Wenlock had not seen Colonel Markham before leaving England, but fortunately had with him his letter of introduction. In a short time a fine, dignified-looking man, in military undress, attended by several persons, was seen through an open glade of the forest approaching the encampment. He advanced with free and easy steps, and saluted Taminent, who received him in a dignified manner. As soon as the first ceremonies were over, Wenlock presented his letter.

"I am truly glad to see you," said Colonel Markham, "and I trust your patron and my good cousin will soon arrive and take the command of the colony."

"It is reported in Upland and the other settlements that his ship is on the way, and will soon be here," said Wenlock.

"I am glad to hear it," said the colonel; "and indeed, I am on my way back, hoping to meet him. But, tell me, who is that pale young man and the two seamen I have observed in the camp."

"They were endeavouring to make their way through the forest, and lost it, as I did," answered Wenlock.

"He speaks truly," said Ford, who crawled up to where the colonel and Wenlock were standing. "I wished to join my friend, that I might, without delay, receive my directions from thee, Colonel Markham," said Ford, "and well-nigh lost my life in the service of my fellow-creatures."

"Well; I doubt not, when Governor Penn arrives due attention will be paid to the merits of all men in the colony," said the colonel. "For my own part, I do not interfere in such matters."

Colonel Markham having spent the remainder of the day at the camp, and rested there during the night, the Englishmen sleeping as securely as if they were in their own country, the whole party set forth for the settlements.

Chapter Eighteen.

Bristol was in those days the chief commercial city of England next to London. It was the centre, too, of a district where large quantities of woollen cloths were manufactured, which were sent forth to foreign lands by the numerous vessels which traded to its port. In a large room belonging to one of the principal merchants in the city, a number of persons were collected. At the head of a long table sat William Penn, while on either side of him were several friends,— Claypole, Moore, Philip Ford, and many others. They were engaged in organising a mercantile company, to which was given the name of the "Free Society of Traders" in Pennsylvania. William Penn, the governor of the new colony, was addressing them.

"I have secured, friends, a number of persons skilful in the manufacture of wool, who have agreed to go forth to our new colony from the valley of Stroud. From the banks of the Rhine, also, many persons conversant with the best modes of cultivating the vine have promised to emigrate."

"We need not fear, then, for the success of our holy enterprise," observed Philip Ford; "and I am ready to embark all my worldly possessions. I have already sent out my beloved son Jonas, a youth of fair promise, and what thing more precious could I stake on the success of our undertaking."

William Penn having made all his arrangements with the new company, giving them very great facilities, returned to London. Here he made preparation for his own departure. It was grievous to him to leave his children and his beloved wife. He hoped, however, in a short time to come back and return with them to the land of his adoption. There was a great stir in the Quaker world, for not only farmers and artisans, but many persons of wealth and education were preparing to take part in the enterprise.

Among the first ships which sailed after the departure of the *Amity*, and those which have before been spoken of, was one, the *Concord*, on board which William Mead and his family, with several friends, set sail for the New World. William Penn saw his old friend off, his prayers going with him, and hoping himself to follow in a short time.

In the autumn of the year 1683, a large vessel might have been seen floating on the waters of the Thames. She was the *Welcome*. Surrounding her were a number of boats which had brought off passengers, while her decks were loaded with bales and packages of every possible description, which the crew were engaged in stowing below. On the deck, also, had been built up sheds for horses and pens for sheep, as also for goats to afford milk, and pigs and poultry in large quantities for provision. Already nearly a hundred persons were collected on board, besides the crew. The signal was given, and the *Welcome* got under weigh to proceed down the Thames. Once more she brought up in the Downs, off Deal. The 1st of September broke bright and clear. Her flags were flying out gaily to the breeze, her white canvas hung to the yards, when a large boat, followed by several smaller ones, came off from the shore, and the young and energetic preacher of the gospel, the governor of a vast province, the originator of the grandest scheme of colonisation ever yet formed, ascended the side of the *Welcome* which was to bear him to the shores of the New World. Prayers ascended from the deck of the proud ship as her anchor was once more lifted, and she proceeded on her voyage to the west. All seemed fair and smiling, and all that forethought and care could arrange had been provided for the passengers. Few who saw William Penn at that moment would have supposed, however, that he was a man of indomitable energy and courage. Downcast and sad, he gazed on the shores of the land he was leaving, which, notwithstanding his general philanthropy, contained those he loved best on earth, where all his tender affections were centred. The Isle of Wight was soon passed. The Land's End faded in the distance, and the stout ship stood across the Atlantic. William Penn soon recovered his energy and spirits, and the captain promised a speedy and prosperous voyage. The governor was walking the deck, talking earnestly with his friend Pearson, a man of large mind and generous heart, when the captain came to them.

"I fear, friends," he said, "that one of our passengers is not long for this world. She has been unwell since she came on board at Deal. Her lips are blue, and dark marks cover her countenance."

The governor and his friend instantly went below; a young girl of some twelve years old lay on her bed in one of the close cabins.

"I fear me much it is the small-pox," said Pearson. "Yet it would be well if we could avoid alarming the other passengers."

The news, however, soon spread, and, alas! so did the disease. Before the next day closed in, the young girl had breathed her last, and her body was committed to the sea. By that time signs of the fearful disorder had appeared on four other persons. The governor, Pearson, and others went about the ship, urging the passengers to air and fumigate their cabins, beseeching them also not to lose courage, and fearlessly visiting those who were already attacked. The sun rose, and ere it sunk again into the ocean, death had claimed two other victims. All this time no sign of alarm was perceptible on the countenance of the governor. He set a noble example to his companions, as, indeed, did his friend Pearson. Perseveringly they went about at all hours of the night and day, attending to the sick, speaking words of comfort to them, and pointing to a Saviour who died to save them; and urging them to put their trust in Him, so that they might not fear, even should they be summoned from the world. It was a time to try all. Some who had appeared weak and nervous before, now exhibited courage and confidence in God's protecting mercy; while others, who had seemed bold and fearless, trembled lest they should be overtaken by the fell disease. Young and old, however, were attacked alike. Day after day one of their number was summoned away, and before the shores of America appeared in sight, thirty-one had fallen victims to the disease. With the change of climate its virulence appeared to cease, and when the *Welcome* sailed up the Delaware, all were convalescent who had escaped its ravages.

The tall ship came to an anchor before Newcastle, and numbers of boats came on to welcome the passengers. Loud shouts arose from the shore when it was known that the long-looked-for governor had arrived. He had lived too long in the world not to be well aware of the importance of appearing to advantage among strangers. He, accompanied by Pearson and the principal friends who had been companions in his voyage, landed in the ship's barge, with flags flying and all the party dressed in their best. He himself appeared in a plain though becoming costume, being distinguished among his companions by his tall and graceful figure, and the blue silk scarf which he wore across his shoulders. It was on the 27th of October, a day memorable in the annals of the colony. As he stepped on shore, old and young of his motley colonists, habited in the costumes of their different nations, crowded forth from their quaint old Dutch and Flemish houses to the shore to meet him. Swedes and Germans—the original settlers—Dutchmen with pipe in mouth, a scattering, albeit, of Scotch everywhere to be found, and English and Welsh in greater numbers. As the party leaving the stately ship reached the land, the crowd on shore opened, and two persons, remarkable for their appearance, with numerous attendants, advanced to the landing-place. One was Colonel Markham, known by his soldier-like bearing, and the handsome uniform of the British army which he still wore. Near him was Wenlock Christison, and Jonas Ford also, who took care to appear among the first in the group. On the other side, a tall figure, his war plumes waving in the breeze, his dress richly ornamented with feathers, his countenance marked with paints of various hue appeared. He was Taminent, the chief of the country, accompanied by a number of his followers of the tribe of Leni-Lenapé. With earnest words of congratulation the governor was welcomed to the land of his adoption by the chief, while Colonel Markham briefly described how far he had carried out his employer's wishes. He had selected a site for the governor's residence, on the Delaware, a few miles below the Falls of Fenton, having purchased the land from the chiefs, who claimed it as their own. He had also laid out the grounds and commenced the building, to which he had given the name of Pennsbury. Then turning to the chief, he said:

"And our brother will bear witness that happily no dispute has taken place between the white men and the natives, while not a drop of blood of either has been shed."

"And while Taminent and his descendants live they will pray the Great Spirit to watch over the white men who have come to their land, and to guard them from all harm," said the chief, taking the governor's hand.

Chapter Nineteen.

As soon as Wenlock could approach the governor, he inquired for his friends, the Meads.

"Have you not seen them?" exclaimed Penn. "Surely the *Concord*, in which they sailed, left England nearly three months ago, and they should have been here for some time already."

"The *Concord* has not arrived," answered Wenlock, and his heart sunk within him.

Every inquiry was made, but none of the vessels which had arrived of late had heard of the *Concord*. Wenlock had been hoping that they might have come out, and almost expected to see them on board the *Welcome*. He was now almost in despair. "I grieve for thee, young man," said the governor; "for I know thy love for my old friend's daughter. I grieve also myself at his loss, if lost he is."

Wenlock was unable to speak in reply.

"The only remedy I can advise for thee, is active employment of body and mind, and the reading of the best of books," added the governor, with a look of compassion at the young man.

Wenlock endeavoured, as far as he could, to follow the advice of his friend. The governor now proceeded up the river, touching on his way at Upland. The inhabitants of the place came out to receive him with delight, a tall pine, which had been allowed to stand when its neighbours were cut away, marking the spot where he went on shore. Turning to Pearson, who had so nobly supported him in his arduous labours among the sick daring the voyage: "What wilt thou, friend, that I should call this place?" he asked.

"Chester, an' it please thee," answered Pearson. "It is my native city, and the affection I bear for it will never be effaced. Yet I might transfer some slight portion to this town."

"Chester, therefore, let it be henceforth called," answered Penn.

While the governor was stopping at the house of Mr Wade, Wenlock went to visit old Rullock, and to see his own humble abode. He found a large party of Dutch emigrants in the town, who had arrived the day before. Among them he recognised a face he knew. Yes, he was certain. It was that of Dr Van Erk.

"Yes, I am indeed myself!" exclaimed the doctor, shaking Wenlock warmly by the hand. "Not knowing by what tyranny we might next be oppressed at home, I resolved to quit the shores of the Old World, and to seek refuge in the New; and my brother agreeing with me, we have come over with our wives and families. He will carry on mercantile pursuits, — and, by the by, he will be glad, I doubt not, to give you employment, — and I shall follow my own profession. My wife and children will, I am sure, be very glad to see you, but as yet we can show you very little hospitality. But you look somewhat sad, my young friend. Tell me what has occurred?"

Wenlock told him the cause of his sadness.

"Well, we will give you all the consolation in our power."

Wenlock felt much pleased at meeting his old friends, and was amply employed, for some time, in obtaining accommodation for them. Every day vessels were arriving with passengers and cargoes, but not one of them brought any account of the *Concord*. His Dutch friends, however, did their utmost to console Wenlock. He thanked them, but yet found his thoughts more than ever going back to Mary. He would have been well-pleased if Ford had kept out of his way, but that person managed to introduce himself to the Van Erks, and he felt sure he was meditating mischief of some sort. The governor then proposed that he should go on a mission on state affairs to Boston, hoping that the change of life and scene might benefit him. Wenlock having received his instructions, accordingly went on board the *Amity*, which vessel, having been thoroughly repaired, was engaged for the purpose.

"But I cannot part from you," exclaimed old Bill Rullock. "I did not think to go to sea again, but if the captain will let me work my passage there and back, I will go along with you."

No arguments would induce the old man to give up his purpose, and Wenlock was not sorry to have so faithful a companion. Rounding Cape May, the *Amity* sailed along the shores of New Jersey, steering to the north, keeping in sight of land till she came off Long Island, forming one side of the magnificent harbour of the New York Bay. Then she stood on, through Massachusetts Bay till the long established city of Boston was reached. Wenlock had expected to meet with kindness and sympathy from the descendants of those who had been driven for conscience' sake to seek a home in the New World. However, even by those to whom he had letters he was received with coldness, and he heard remarks made about Quakers generally, and himself especially, which somewhat tried his temper. His name, too, seemed especially to excite anger among the citizens. At length he was summoned to appear before the governor of the state.

"Know you not, young man, that we allow no persons of your persuasion to remain in our state?" exclaimed the governor. "There was one, of your name too, banished not long since; and some who have ventured to return, have of necessity been put to death, as breakers of the law and rebels against the state."

"Verily, I knew not that such was the case," answered Wenlock; "and when I have performed my business here, I am ready to take my departure. I have never been here before, and truly I should be glad to hear of one of my name, hoping that he might prove a relative; for at present I know not any one to whom I am kith and kin."

"Stand aside, young man, and bring forth the prisoner, with whose trial we will proceed," exclaimed the governor, casting a frowning glance at Wenlock.

The governor was proceeding to condemn the prisoner, when a loud voice was heard, exclaiming, "Pronounce not judgment." Wenlock started, and looked towards the speaker. He almost fancied that he saw his father standing before him.

"Who are you, who thus dares to interrupt the court?" exclaimed the governor.

"I am Wenlock Christison," was the answer. "I come to prevent you from condemning the innocent."

"Then thou art my uncle!" exclaimed Wenlock, hurrying towards him. "I know thee by thy likeness to my father."

"And, verily, I know thee," exclaimed the old man. "And what is thy name?"

"Thine own," answered Wenlock.

"Carry them both off to prison. They will hang together well," exclaimed the governor.

In spite of Wenlock's protestations that he had been sent in the character of an envoy by the governor of the new state, he and his uncle were committed to prison. The old man, however, seemed but little concerned at this.

"We shall be set at liberty ere long, nephew," he said; "and I rejoice greatly to have at length found thee, and more than all, that thou hast embraced the true and perfect way of life."

Bill Rullock, on hearing what had occurred, was very indignant, and, almost forgetting that he himself had become a Quaker, was about to attempt forcibly to liberate his friend.

The governor kept Wenlock shut up, but seemed doubtful about proceeding with him. His uncle was, however, brought up day after day, refusing to acknowledge himself guilty, warning his persecutors of the punishment which was soon to overtake them. Old Rullock employed himself in making interest with various people in the place, to obtain the liberation of his friend, warning them that though Master William Penn might not take vengeance on them, there was a certain Colonel Markham, who would be influenced by no such scruples. The result was, that not only young Wenlock, but old Christison, was set at liberty.

"Nephew, I have wealth," exclaimed his uncle, "and I rejoice to find one who will inherit it. However, of one thing I am resolved, not to spend it among this people. The account thou dost give me of the new colony has made me resolve to go and end my days there; and we will together leave in the vessel that brought thee hither, as soon as she is ready to sail."

Although the Friends were no longer persecuted at Boston, as may be supposed, it was not a pleasant city for them to reside in. A considerable number, therefore, set sail on board the *Amity*, which had a prosperous voyage to the Delaware.

Chapter Twenty.

We left the *Amity* sailing up the Delaware. During her absence, a number of vessels had arrived both from England and from Dutch and German ports, and it pleasant to those interested in the welfare of the colony to see them land their passengers and cargoes, the former often collected in picturesque spots on the banks, under the shelter of white tents, yellow wigwams, dark brown log huts, and sometime green arbours of boughs. Off Chester a shattered weather-beaten bark was seen at anchor. Here also the *Amity* came to an anchor, although news was brought on board that the governor had already selected the site of his capital on the point of land at the junction of the Delaware and the Schuylkill. Wenlock turned his eyes towards the shattered vessel, and naturally inquired who she was.

"Oh, she is the long lost *Concord!*" was the answer.

Wild agitation filled his bosom as he heard these words, but it was succeeded by fear.

"What have become of the passengers, then?" he asked.

"Some of them died, but others arrived in her. She was cast away on an island, and only with great difficulty was at length got off."

"But where are they?" asked Wenlock.

"Most of them are at Chester, though some have gone off to the new city," was the answer.

Unable to obtain any further information, Wenlock jumped into the first boat returning on shore. He bethought him that he would at once go to his friend, Dr Van Erk, who would be more likely than any one else to give him information. He inquired for his house. Wealth will do much. While others were lodged in huts, the doctor had already secured a comfortable residence for his family. Wenlock hurried towards it, but before he reached it he met the doctor. After they had greeted each other, he told him of whom he was in search.

"Come, my young friend, and perhaps we may find them." The doctor took his arm and led him along till they reached a somewhat highly-pointed but very neat cottage.

"There, whom do you see there?" he asked, pointing through the window. There were four ladies, two old ones and two young. One of them was Gretchen. She was close to the window, so he saw her first; but beyond her,—yes, there was no doubt about it, there sat Mary Mead. They were engaged in their work, so they did not see him.

"Stay," said the doctor, "I forgot. A certain friend of yours has been telling them that you are dead; that he has had news of it; and it might agitate them somewhat, if you were to appear suddenly. I will go in and prepare them." Wenlock stood outside, hid by the porch. He heard first Master Mead's rich voice utter a note of surprise, and then several female voices. He thought he could distinguish Mary's. It was very low, though. Master Mead was the first to come out and welcome him, and in a few seconds he was in the presence of Mary and Gretchen and the two old ladies.

"My dear sister, I am so thankful," exclaimed Gretchen, bestowing a kiss on Mary, "that he has been restored to you." Whatever doubt Master Mead had before, as to bestowing his daughter on Wenlock, it was set at rest by the appearance of the elder Wenlock Christison, who very speedily satisfied all prudential scruples, by informing the worthy father of his intentions regarding his nephew.

While the party were assembled, *a head was put into the door*. It was quickly withdrawn.

"Oh! it is that odious Jonas Ford," said Gretchen. "I am sure he never comes here to speak truth."

"Nay; but we should not think harshly of a friend," observed Mead.

"I do not think over harshly," answered Gretchen. "If ever there was a sleek hypocrite, that man is one." Time showed that Gretchen was right, although Wenlock escaped the consequences of his machinations. Wenlock, however, could not remain long at Chester, having to proceed up to the new capital, Philadelphia, to give an account of his mission to the governor. He was received in the kindest manner by the governor, who was living in a log hut while his intended residence, some way higher up, was building.

"Here, my young friend," he said, pointing to a large sheet of paper spread out on a table, "is the plan of our future capital. See, we shall have two noble rows of houses fronting the two rivers; and, here, a magnificent avenue of one hundred feet in width, which we will call the High Street, uniting them with lines of trees on either side. Then we will have Broad Street, cutting the city in two parts from north to south, with a magnificent square of ten acres in the centre, and in the middle of each quarter there shall be another square, each of eight acres, for the recreation of the people, and we will have many detached buildings covered with trailing plants, green and rural, to remind us of the country towns of England. Already many houses have been put up, and the people show a commendable energy in erecting more, as fast as materials can be procured. To-morrow I have appointed for a meeting with the native chiefs, to hold a solemn conference for the purpose of confirming former treaties, and forming with them a lasting league of peace and friendship. I am glad that thou art come, Christison, as it will be a matter of great interest. Thou hast probably visited the spot with my kinsman, Colonel Markham. It is called Sakimaxing, the meaning of which is, 'The place or locality of kings.'"

"Yea," answered Wenlock; "I accompanied him on more than one occasion, when he had to make arrangements with Taminent. The natives hold in great respect an ancient elm of vast size which, they say, is already one hundred and fifty-five years old. Under its branches the tribes are wont to meet to smoke the calumet of peace, and to arrange their disputes."

"No fitter spot could have been chosen," observed Penn. "We hope, too, that they will ever be ready to smoke with us the calumet of peace."

At an early hour the following morning, the governor, with his faithful friend Pearson, and other attendants, men of influence among the settlers, set forth on horseback to a spot where the conference was to take place. It was an open space, close to the banks of the magnificent Delaware. In the centre stood the stately council elm, spreading its branches far and wide over the green turf. Circling round was the primeval forest, with the dark cedar, the tall pine, the shining chestnut, and the bright maple, and many other trees, stretching far away inland. The governor and his companions, leaving their horses, advanced towards the meeting-place. His tall and graceful figure was especially distinguished by the light-blue sash he wore, as a simple mark by which the natives of the forest might recognise him. He had never affected ultra-plainness in dress, preferring rather to simplify the costume which he had hitherto worn. His outer coat was long, covered, as was the custom, with buttons. An ample waistcoat of rich material, with full trousers, slashed at the sides and tied with ribbons, while his shirt had a profusion of handsome ruffles, and a hat of the form worn in his younger days, completed his costume. On one side was Colonel Markham, already well known to the natives, and on the other his faithful friend Pearson; while Wenlock and his other companions came a little way behind them. As they advanced, the Indians were seen to approach, led by Taminent, their chief, all habited in the ancient costume of the forest, with the brightest of feathers, their faces painted in their most gorgeous style. A number of the settlers from various parts had followed the governor, and now formed a circle at a respectful distance. No monarchs of the Old World could have behaved with more dignity than did the Indian chief and the Quaker governor. Taminent having retired and consulted with his councillors, again advanced, placing on his own head a chaplet, in which was fastened a small horn, the symbol of his power. Whenever a chief of the Leni-Lenapé placed on his brow this chaplet, the spot was made sacred, and all present inviolable. The chief then seated himself with his councillors on either side, the older warriors ranging themselves in the form of a crescent round them, the younger forming an outer semicircle. The English governor then arose, the handsomest and most graceful of all present, and addressed the natives in their own language. He told them that they had one common Father, who reigns above; and that his desire was that his people, and theirs should be brothers, and that as brothers and friends they should treat each other, and that thus they should help each other against all who would do them harm. And, lastly, that both his people and the Leni-Lenapé should tell their children of this league and bond of friendship which had been formed,—that it might grow stronger and stronger, and be kept bright and clean, as long as the waters should run down the creeks and rivers, and the sun and moon and stars endure. He then laid the scroll containing the proposed treaty on the ground, which was accepted by Taminent, and preserved for ages afterwards by the Indians. Thus was this treaty ratified with a "Yea, yea,"—the only treaty, as has been remarked, known in the world, never sworn to, and never broken. Thus was Pennsylvania happily founded without injustice, without bloodshed, without crime; and, blessed by Heaven, continued to flourish, the most happy and prosperous colony ever formed by Britons.

Our tale is ended. A faint outline of the history of a true hero has been traced. From it may be learned in what true heroism consists. William Penn (for he is our real hero), like the Master he served, though in the world, was not of it. He, as all must who desire to be faithful subjects of the Lord Jesus Christ, and not mere nominal Christians, took Him as his example. He had counted the cost, and entered boldly on the warfare. Worldly honours and distinctions were given up, though the highest were within his grasp. Persecution and contempt were willingly accepted; imprisonment endured without murmuring. He trusted to One all-powerful to help in time of need. His firm faith even in this life was rewarded. He was enabled to overcome the world.

A True Hero

So will it be with all who like William Penn, know in whom they trust, if they persevere like him without wavering.

The End.